THE BAREKNUCKLE GROOM

The Thompsons of Locust Street

HOLLY BUSH

Holly Bush Books

CHAPTER 1

December 1868

PHILADELPHIA

JAMES THOMPSON EYED THE DAINTY BRUNETTE AND THE others as they approached him. She was dressed in festive colors with matching ribbons, sparkling up at him, her lashes fluttering, her cheeks pink. He was at some infernal gathering, one of many that the Pendergast family hosted, being a prominent Philadelphia family, though not as snobby and stuck on themselves as he'd expected when his sister Elspeth had first taken an interest in her husband, Alexander Pendergast.

But the guests at their parties were exactly the kind of people James expected them to be, including the brunette, the two men on either side of her, one of them puffing out his chest, and certainly the tall blond goddess with the wide pink lips and pale blue eyes. She looked at him as if he were the lowliest of the low, barely a servant, one of the unwashed, or even a beggar. He did not know how a woman could convey so much disdain for a person with a smile, but this woman did exactly that.

And he had plenty of experience with women. He loved women, and they loved him. It mattered little if they were tall or short or brunette or red-headed or coltishly thin or buxom. He loved them all. But those women were young widows or ones he met at the clubs he frequented or just women working at one of the many factories and offices in Philadelphia, his home since the age of eleven, when he'd come from Scotland with his family. They were definitely not the women at this party. A quick toss with any of these women would not happen, and if it did, exile to some remote location would be expected shortly thereafter or worse, marriage.

Alexander and Elspeth joined the group, and his sister kissed his cheek. "Thank you for coming, James."

He smiled down at her. She was the very picture of happiness and health, bright-eyed, blushing, and pretty, dressed as if she were royalty. Her husband gazed at her and patted her hand where it lay on his arm. He doted on her, and James was glad of it. Being the middle child in a large family, and the first to marry and leave the nest, could be daunting. She'd also been the victim of violence. Elspeth deserved Alexander's adulation.

"I was telling my friends that you're a famous boxer, Mr. Thompson," the brunette tittered.

"Let me introduce you, James," Alexander said, nodding to the brunette. "Miss Gladys Bartholomew, Mr. John Williams, Mr. Alfred Dundermore, and Miss Lucinda Vermeal, or should I say Mademoiselle de Vermeal?" Alex said and turned to James. "Mr. James Thompson. My lovely bride's eldest brother."

James nodded to the two women and shook the hands of the men. John Williams folded his arms across his chest. "I've always been told that these bareknuckle matches are a setup, just theater, with a winner determined ahead of the match."

Alexander chuckled. "Hardly, John. You'll have to come with

me the next time James is fighting. It's quite real and still very entertaining."

"That sounds fair enough," Williams said and looked at Dundermore. "Will you join us if we go? Could be an interesting evening."

Dundermore yawned against the back of his hand. "I can't see how that would be very interesting. And anyway, I'm usually busy at the Philadelphia Historical Club since my father has been the president these last five years. I rarely have time for frivolity."

James smirked and stared at Dundermore until the man looked away. He turned to Williams. "I make sure Alexander and his father have tickets for my bouts. I can easily get one for you as well, if you're interested."

"May I come too?" Gladys asked and leaned toward him.

"I don't think you'd like it," Elspeth said, shaking her head. "I saw him fight once, and that was enough!"

"Women aren't welcome by the crowds that pay to see a match, and I don't think it would be safe, Miss Bartholomew." He smiled at her. "I couldn't just step out of the ring if there was some unruly man bothering you, now could I?"

"Oh," she said with a giggle and waved her red-and-white striped fan in front of her face. "I suppose not."

The ice-cold one, Miss Vermeal, in her pale blue silk dress, with diamonds at her ears, wrists, and neck, checked herself before she rolled her eyes at Miss Bartholomew, but James saw her smirk even if it was not visible to others. Her eyes were revealing, he thought as she turned to look at him, as if she knew he saw her subtlety and didn't care. He was of little value and certainly of no consequence. He would like to show her his *consequence*, he thought, the bawdy comment ringing in his head. He could not deny that she was alluring.

"Would you care to dance, Miss Bartholomew?" Williams asked.

The woman cast a coy glance at James before turning to

Williams with a smile and fluttering lashes. "It would be my honor, Mr. Williams."

"Mrs. Pendergast," Dundermore intoned. "With your husband's permission, would you be so kind as to grace me with your hand for the dance floor?"

James caught Alexander's pursed lips and raised brows and hid a smile. As if Alexander could stop Elspeth, or any of his sisters, if they really wanted to do something. Alexander would have said just that when Elspeth replied.

"Certainly, Mr. Dundermore. I am very interested to hear of your work with the Philadelphia Historical Society."

"Excellent, Mrs. Pendergast," he said and winged his arm to her. "You'll have to tell me how you and your worthy husband met."

James laughed as the couple walked to the dance floor, thinking of the day that Alexander and Elspeth had met in front of the whorehouse near Mrs. Fendale's hat shop. He belatedly realized that it was just he, Alexander, and Miss Vermeal still standing together. She was gazing serenely at the dancers as they took their places for a waltz. Alexander was gesturing to the dance floor, intending, it seemed, to partner with her when Graham, the Pendergast head of security, stepped between him and Miss Vermeal.

"Ah, pardon me," Alexander said. "Duty calls."

James watched Alexander walk away and blew out a breath. "Well, I suppose that means you are stuck dancing with me."

Miss Vermeal did not turn her head. "Or we could casually step away from each other, thereby negating the necessity for either of us to feel any obligation."

"What if I want to dance with you because you are a beautiful woman who I'd like to hold in my arms, even if it is in the very public setting of this dance floor?"

She glanced at him with no expression on her face or in those pale blue eyes. "You've said that word, beautiful, based on a fallacious belief. Do you know what that word means? Fallacious? Would you like me to explain it to you?"

James stepped close to her and touched her elbow. "There is no mistaken belief in the idea that you are beautiful. You are."

"The mistaken belief is that you think I care for your compliments or good opinion, Mr. Thompson."

He smiled at her and waited until her eyes drifted away from his. "Dance with me, Miss Vermeal."

She huffed a little breath of annoyance. "I suppose I must as you've been holding my arm for several moments and others are beginning to notice." She moved away from his hand, turned, and walked toward the dance floor. She glanced over her shoulder. "Mr. Thompson," she said loudly enough that several heads turned. "Do you no longer wish to dance with me, sir?"

JAMES THOMPSON SMILED AT HER, JUST ONE SIDE OF THAT FULL mouth of his lifting up, revealing deep dimples and a small chip on the corner of his front tooth. It was a devastating smile, she thought, and men smiled at her all the time and she was rarely, if ever, affected. He was not as easily manipulated as she was accustomed to, but then she'd never known a boxer before. How gauche! It was if she were dancing with Laurent, the Vermeal butler!

Thompson slid a hand around her waist and grasped her hand with his—calloused, strong, and large. She laid her palm on his shoulder and felt muscles bunch under her fingers. It was a wonder his finely made jacket did not split its seams. She was used to an entirely different sort of man. Her father was tall and slender, still handsome, even though he'd been a widower for nearly twenty years.

All the men she'd known in Virginia before her father had moved them to Philadelphia earlier in the year were the same. They were property owners and intellectuals, well-bred and mannered, certainly not working men. But even so, her father felt Philadelphia was more properly able to introduce his only daughter to a higher and more sophisticated society than what Virginia had been able to. He was sure his gem, his diamond, would be admired and courted and much sought after in the city of brotherly love. And she was! She was courted and admired until she was bored to tears. There was nothing authentic about her swains' regard; she was a pretty—some said beautiful—prize with scads of money and a family history of French royalty and influencers. She knew exactly what they were after: aligning themselves with Henri Vermeal, his tobacco money, and his vast properties in America and Europe.

This man, *this James Thompson*, she said to herself, was nothing like any of the other men she knew, probably because they didn't go around smashing their fists into another man's nose to support themselves. But there was another difference. He was focused on her in a way she was unaccustomed to. His eyes had not left her face, his intense gaze slightly mocking. Even the chipped tooth and the stitch-mark scar she could see near his mouth, as she was close enough now to notice, did not detract from how handsome he was. In fact, his beauty was enhanced by those imperfections, turning a perfect face into a wildly attractive one. She felt a little breathless. A little overwhelmed. Not that she'd allow this ruffian to know he'd unnerved her.

The music began, and he pulled her closer than was proper as they made the first turn. "A little more distance between us, Mr. Thompson."

"Not playing the mistreated innocent now, are we?" he said, smiling and taking the sting out of his comment. He raised the pitch of his voice to mock her. "Do you no longer wish to dance with me, sir?"

He looked at her directly, raising his brows. She had no excuse for playing the maligned young woman other than to put him in his rightful place, which was not holding her this closely in his well-muscled arms. "Careful, Mr. Thompson. High society isn't a place you can just go about punching people that you don't like. It calls for a degree of subtlety."

He barked a laugh, making her feel as if she might enjoy his brand of happiness, if it didn't make her breathless, as it did now. He pulled his hand holding hers to his eyes, wiping away his tears on the back of his knuckles. It was a startling intimacy. She stared at their joined hands for a moment before bringing her eyes back to his. There was a lazy confidence there that she did not care for, although she was certain there was little she could say or do to change it.

"I hear a bit of the south in your speech, Miss Vermeal. Are you new to Philadelphia?"

"I am, Mr. Thompson. My father moved us from Virginia last spring."

"Business interests?"

"Some," she replied. "Mostly, he wanted me to benefit from the more formal society that Philadelphia had to offer, although as I'm dancing a waltz with a common street fighter, it seems his hopes were not fulfilled."

His eyes narrowed, and his lips thinned. A hit, she thought triumphantly.

"I am not a street fighter, miss. I'm a boxer. There's a difference."

"Really? How strange. I thought both occupations, if you could call them that, involved bloodying another's face so the riffraff had something to entertain them and spend their coins on instead of on food for their families."

He whirled her through a series of quick turns, weaving in and out of other couples. She did not miss a step, and when he finally slowed, she raised her brows at him.

"Why, Miss Vermeal, it's almost as if you intend for me to judge you as a snob. Perhaps you'd like to share some of those glittering diamonds around that long white neck of yours with the poor wives waiting at home for their men to bring home bread when they've wasted all of their coins on a fight."

"Gambling is always a waste, Mr. Thompson."

He hitched up the side of his mouth. "Not true. When the riffraff bet on me, they're always the winner. I don't lose."

The music stopped, and he continued to hold her, even as others left the dance floor.

"May I escort you to your family?"

"No," she said and removed her hand from his shoulder and her other from his grip. "I can find my own way, Mr. Thompson. You are quite superfluous."

Thompson shoved his hands into his pants pockets, quite an ungentlemanly thing to do, and smiled at her. He was, she thought as she turned away, the most handsome man she'd ever seen.

CHAPTER 2

James watched Lucinda Vermeal wander away. She was truly elegant in her conceit, he thought, but damn if she didn't fit perfectly in his arms. Nearly as tall as him, with a long, elegant neck, sultry eyes with thick fair lashes, and lips meant to be kissed. But she was definitely not for him. She would need constant attention and adoration, as she was evidently already accustomed to, which he was not willing to provide.

He turned and spied his youngest sister, Kirsty, with a group including Alexander's sister, Annabelle Pendergast, who, if he was not mistaken—and he didn't believe he was—had developed an interest in him. He had no intention of encouraging her. She was a beautiful and bright young woman, but he felt ancient beside her, and she was in constant company with his younger sister, which didn't feel right somehow. And she was Alexander's sister. He was bored quickly when he'd stepped out with the same woman a few times, and he'd end up breaking Annabelle's heart, and then Alexander would try and break his nose, and he'd have to beat his brother-in-law to a pulp, which would make Elspeth hate him for all time. No. He wasn't going to risk any of that. He'd be politely distant.

"James! James!" Kirsty said as he approached. He could not help but smile at his her. She was a happy and loving young woman, if occasionally hasty in her actions and words, and she was dear to him. He kissed her cheek when he was beside her.

"You're looking lovely tonight, Kirsty," he said. "You haven't sat out a dance as far as I could tell."

"I haven't! I've danced them all!" she said and turned to include Annabelle, who was red in the face and looking down at her hands. "Doesn't Annabelle look lovely too?"

"Of course she does," he replied and nodded to her. "All you young ladies look nice. That's why all these young men are gathered around you."

"Oh, James, but don't you think Anna—" She jumped and closed her mouth when he pinched her arm.

Fortunately, a young man asked Annabelle to dance. She glanced up at James as if waiting for him to tell the man the next dance was his. He was saved when another of the men gathered around Kirsty and Annabelle asked him a question.

"Was that Miss Vermeal you were dancing with earlier?"

"Yes, I danced with her."

"Who is Miss Vermeal?" Kirsty asked.

"Just the most beautiful . . ." one of the men began. "Present company excepted."

"She has the bluest eyes."

"And that dress she has on," another one said but quickly closed his mouth.

"Gentlemen," James smiled slowly, "you fellows just leave Miss Vermeal to me. She enjoyed our dance, I'm certain." He winked.

There was a collective male sigh of jealousy, and maybe he'd said just enough to make Annabelle believe he'd set his sights on another woman. James bid them good night, found Alexander's parents to thank them for inviting him, and slipped out a side door. He'd find MacAvoy and head to the tavern they frequented for a cold ale and any news of his upcoming opponent.

. . .

JAMES SAT AT A TABLE NEAR THE BACK OF THE WATER STREET Tavern. He watched the comings and goings, the men leaving with women, the women refusing to leave with men, and the barkeep making a coin on everyone, happy or sad. Daisy, the serving girl, leaned over him, putting one very fine breast within inches of his lips. He smiled.

"Not tonight, darling," he said and kissed her neck with a loud smacking sound.

"Oh, James," she said as she straightened and tilted her head at him with a smile. "When are you going to make an honest woman of me? You know you'd like to find me in your bed every night."

He slapped her ass lightly. "Ah, Daisy, but I'd never know whose bed you'd just left!"

"There is that, James," she said in a wistful voice and picked up her tray. "Men just love me. Another brew?"

James nodded and watched her walk away as MacAvoy slid into the chair opposite him.

"Where have you been?" James asked. "I thought we said eleven."

The only man he trusted to work his corner of any boxing ring and his oldest friend blushed. "Eleanor's been having trouble getting Mary into bed, and that darling little girl just loves me. She falls asleep in my arms."

"You were at Alexander's?"

"One of the maids was going to sit with Mary once she was asleep, and Eleanor and I were going to take a walk and maybe have some pie at the coffee shop. But once Mary saw me, she would not let us leave, and when that girl looks at me with those beautiful brown eyes and puts her little arms around my neck, well, I can't be worried about having an ale with you."

Eleanor Emory was Alexander and Elspeth's housekeeper. He

and MacAvoy met her when Alexander had taken them to his home after the three of them had found some trouble and needed a few cuts cleaned up. MacAvoy had immediately been enamored with the pretty widow, but it had taken him nearly six months to get up the courage to ask her if he might take her to the theater. James remembered it clearly, as MacAvoy had droned on and on with nerves before he finally took himself off to ask the woman.

"You better be careful, Malcom," James said. "She don't seem the type to be casual about a man, and Elspeth adores her and Mary. She'll have your hide when you move on, mark my words, and you know Elspeth can be a spitfire when she gets her back up."

MacAvoy took a long pull on his ale and looked out at the crowd in the tavern. "How do you know I'll want to move on?"

"Don't be a nodcock. We've been friends since we were boys and have spent the last five years chasing plenty of skirts. It won't mean anything."

MacAvoy swallowed and took a deep breath. "I want to marry her. With this last promotion at the mill, my cut of the prize money, and some work on the side with the Pendergasts' security men, I've been able to put away some coin. I can afford a small house."

"You want to marry her? That's shit. You're just trying to get under her skirts. What? She won't let you there without a ring? Move on! There's plenty of pretty skirts to get under."

MacAvoy shook his head. "You don't get it, James. This isn't a game to me. I love her and her little girl."

"Did she give you some cockamamie line about being a good, virtuous woman? What shit. She's just another pussy," James said and picked up his ale. He did not hold it long. MacAvoy knocked it out of his hand and pulled him up from his seat by his jacket.

"Don't you ever talk about her that way. I mean it, James. I know you could beat me to a bloody pulp, but that don't mean I will allow you to talk about her in that disrespectful way. I won't. We can take it outside, or you can apologize."

The tavern crowd had gone completely quiet, and the barkeep picked up the long wooden plank he called "the peacekeeper." James dropped back into his seat, staring at MacAvoy, who was breathing hard, now towering over him with both clenched fists leaning on the tabletop.

"Sit down, Malcolm. I'm sorry I made light of the woman's virtue."

MacAvoy dropped into his chair, staring out at the crowd, now turning back to their own drinks and conversations. His foot was tapping, and he cracked his knuckles. He turned to James.

"I've an early morning tomorrow," he said as he rose.

"Wait," James said. "We were going to talk about what you found out about Crankshaw."

"It'll keep. We can meet next week."

James watched him go. He'd screwed that up, hadn't he, he thought to himself. His best friend, as loyal as a brother, insulted so deeply the man didn't even want to talk about what was more important to them than anything. Boxing. They lived and breathed it. MacAvoy set up the fights, scouted the opponents, negotiated the prize money, and James arrived on the appointed night and did what he did best. Beat the living hell out of another man. MacAvoy also made sure James worked to keep his stamina up and build more muscle too, forcing him to focus on his training.

They told each other everything worth telling. And now Malcom had confessed something that was most likely hard for him to admit and he'd been nothing but dismissive. There was some very small part of James that was a bit jealous too, although he'd never admit that to another soul. But the idea that MacAvoy had found a partnership that might exclude him left a bitter taste in his mouth. He fished a coin out of his pocket for Daisy, tossed it on the table, and left to find his bed.

* * *

LUCINDA KISSED HER FATHER'S CHEEK AFTER COMING INTO THE
small dining room used by the family for their morning meals in
their mansion in the most exclusive neighborhood of Philadelphia. He was holding a newspaper in one hand and a cup of
coffee in the other.

"Good morning, Papa."

"Good morning, Lucinda," he said and stood, never removing
his eyes from what he was reading.

"Good morning, Aunt," she said.

"Good morning, dear," Aunt Louisa said as she contemplated
the food on her fork.

Lucinda wandered to the buffet and chose her plate, waiting
for the young man wearing the livery of another time, including
stockings, white breeches, an embroidered red vest and coat, and
buckled shoes, to fill her plate. Her father insisted all the household staff be attired not only formally, but in clothing from the
previous century. But she did not complain. He was good to her,
even though his insistence on formal behavior and mores was
unfortunate and sometimes embarrassing.

Their current home and Chateau Vermeal in Virginia, where
they'd lived until the previous spring, were decorated much like
what her father remembered of the family's homes in Spain and
included some of the artwork from there. His and Aunt Louisa's
parents, Lucinda's grandparents, a young couple both of royal
blood, had somehow escaped the Reign of Terror in their remote
locale and maintained their vast inherited wealth at the same
time. But being prudent, and realizing that the changes in France,
including the rise of Napoleon, would not be peaceful or profitable for the Vermeals, they began to ship priceless artwork and
artifacts to Spain and amassed trunk after trunk of gold coins.
Telling a few trusted neighbors and friends that they intended to
enjoy a holiday in Italy, they had promptly sailed for Spain with

the clothes on their backs and heavy trunks, not full of clothing and personal effects, but rather precious metal. Her grandpapa had reportedly said that replacing wardrobes would be the least of their problems.

They settled in the port town of Barcelona, where her grandpapa made a second fortune in shipping and her grandmother birthed two children. As a young man in the 1840s, her papa recognized the opportunities to expand his wealth in America and brought his French-born bride from a family visiting the city, to Virginia, raising tobacco and other crops, and straddled the coming Civil War by divesting himself of slaves and contributing gold and goods heavily to both sides. Marie Vermeal died giving birth to a boy when Lucinda was just two years old, and her brother lived only a few hours. Aunt Louisa was sent for to care for her brother's daughter and dutifully put aside her own life to raise her niece. She was the only mother Lucinda could remember.

Lucinda took her seat while another young man helped her with her chair, his eyes appropriately downcast. The plate of her favorite foods was sat before her and steaming tea poured into the hand-painted china cup to her right. She dropped in one sugar cube and stirred.

"How is everyone this morning?" she asked.

Papa ruffled his papers but did not reply. Aunt Louisa stared at her.

"Is something amiss?" she said quietly to her aunt. "Something with Papa's business?"

"No. I believe your father's business continues to prosper. I recently met with his man of business, and my accounts continue to expand."

Oddly forward thinking, Father had given his sister a share of the Vermeal companies' profits since she'd come to America. Or perhaps she'd demanded it, knowing she'd be giving up her chances to marry and have children of her own. Maybe she wouldn't have come otherwise. Lucinda had never had the courage to ask her, and didn't her father always say it was crass to talk about money?

Lucinda sipped her tea and slathered the warm roll in her hand with apricot preserves, her favorite. She looked up when her father put his paper down in a rumble.

"What is it?" she asked to his stern face. He was rarely angry, but she thought he might be now.

"I blame your aunt." He signaled the servants to leave the room.

"Blame her for what, Papa? What has happened?"

"There was nothing untoward about Lucinda's behavior or mine," Aunt said.

"Clearly, that is not the case."

"What are you talking about?" Lucinda asked.

"I know you've done it, girl, there is no use acting the inno-cent. Not only did Gauteau visit me already this morning, but your aunt admitted as much!"

"Please tell me what you are talking about, Papa."

"Do not turn on the tears, dear. I'm quite immune to them when it comes to the family's honor."

Lucinda took a deep breath and calmed herself as much as she was able, although she was nowhere near tears. "Family honor?"

Father began to bellow, but Aunt shushed him. "One of your dance partners made comments about your dance together. I watched you the entire time, and there was nothing, well, nothing that should invoke this level of hysteria."

"Hysteria, Louisa? Hysteria? She is a Vermeal! Meant to partner in marriage with someone of status. There's no royalty in America, more's the pity, but there is a ruling class nonetheless. She is meant to carry the family name to a marriage with one of the sons of that class and raise children worthy of this family."

"You're making far too much of this, Henri," Aunt said and dabbed her mouth with the linen serviette.

"Would someone please tell me what you believe I have done?" she asked.

Papa scorched her with a glare. "You danced with a man last night who is not worthy of your notice. A man Gauteau has told me is nothing more than a common street fighter, from a family with a secretive history, no doubt born of some shame. From Scotland, of all places!"

Her mind buzzed, noting that her father had called James Thompson the exact same thing she had called him, and that name had set him on edge. "I was introduced by Mr. Pendergast's son. James Thompson is his wife's brother."

"Sad for that family, then, that they have aligned themselves with that sort. The Pendergasts, I understand, are a notable Philadelphia family. The son's connection cheapens them."

"Papa. We danced one dance."

"And he held you very close, from what I've been told."

"No more than any other young man I've partnered with," she said. She would not share that she'd told him to loosen his hold on her. No use upsetting him more than he already was.

Papa slammed his fist down on the table, making the china jump. "But that is not all! He bandied your name about to other men there, bragging that he'd more than danced with you, implying something devious and not fit for a lady's ears."

"He what?"

"He spoke to some young people after your dance and said something to the effect of his winning your affections and that other men should stay away from you. He may have just been bragging, and he certainly looked like a man who was confident. It was also said that you enjoyed yourself very much while in his arms," Aunt said.

"Must you be so crude, Louisa?"

"Crude? What was crude, Henri? My use of the word 'arms'?"

"It is indelicate, especially in front of an unwed young woman to be speaking of . . . parts of one's body."

Louisa smiled at her brother. "I am to this day unwed. Having left behind a young man in Spain, to do my duty to my older brother and to my family. Not that I regret a moment of my time raising your daughter, but I assumed you would remarry shortly after Marie's death and that I would be free to pursue my own life. And now, after these twenty years, you accuse me of crude behavior?" Aunt Louisa stood, picked up her teacup, and went to the door of the breakfast room. "You will miss me when I'm gone, Henri."

The door closed softly as Lucinda looked at her father. "I just danced with him."

"I brought you to this city to begin the extraordinary task of carrying on the next generation of Vermeals, even though your children will not carry our name. You will have incredible wealth when I am gone. And influence in European capitals. Your behavior must be beyond reproach. The choice of your partner, your husband, must be someone up to the task of international business and a wide range of philanthropic interests, meant to carry the name, Vermeal Industries, forward for generations. He must be well-bred and educated, nothing less than one of the British schools for college, although Harvard would do, I suppose."

"You have planned this out? Will my inclinations be considered?"

"Young women have been doing their duty to their families since the beginning of time. This is not something new, Lucinda. If your personal inclinations coincide with the man best suited to be your husband, it would be for the better, although those inclinations cannot divert us from our ultimate goal. There is no reason to think that I won't be here for many years to come, maintaining the family and fortune. Of course, I have written into my will that you will inherit control of much of the Vermeal wealth. Blood tells, as you know, and I can't risk our heritage on a young man who may turn to drink or to the church, God forbid, or to any distraction that would not be suitable for the Vermeal family. As you can see, I'm entrusting you with great responsibility and power when your aunt and I are gone. A heady gift for a young woman."

Lucinda listened to her father with something akin to horror. She'd always known that he wanted her to make a good and respectable marriage—of course he did. He was her father and loved her. But this speech, this recounting of settled decisions, peeled away any notions that she may find happiness in her choice of husband. The characteristics that she would hope for would not be considered.

"And where do you think you will find this paragon of manhood who will meet all of your requirements for family and education and business skills, who will be controlled by his papa-in-law and usurped by his wife when you are gone? What kind of man would agree to such a plan?"

"He won't know all the details, my dear. That would be short-sighted. And I doubt any young man would turn away from your beauty and virtue. You are a 'diamond of the first water,' as the British say about their most sought-after marriageable daughters. There is not a man with normal tendencies that would not wish you to be the mother of his children."

"And much like the future son-in-law who will be kept in the dark, you've not been forthcoming with me either."

"I'm telling you now, Lucinda. You are ready to know and understand your role." He looked over his spectacles at her. "I will concede you were not at fault by dancing with this street ruffian, as he was introduced to you by the host, but you must be considerably more discerning, more circumspect, in the future."

She looked down at her plate of congealed eggs and cold toasted bread. Even the apricot preserves looked unappetizing. Her father did not look at her as she stood, never taking his eyes from the newspaper he was now reading. She walked to the door, her mind and feelings a jumble, and turned back to her beloved father.

"He is not a street fighter, you know; he is a boxer. There is a difference."

She could still hear his shouts as she climbed the steps to her room.

CHAPTER 3

"Did you enjoy the party last night, Kirsty?" Aunt Murdoch asked as they sat down together for the Thompson Sunday dinner after church, the oldest sister, Muireall, at the head and their great aunt, who'd made the trek with the family back in 1855, at the foot. Payden, the youngest, sat beside James and Kirsty, Elspeth and Alexander sat across the table from him. Mrs. McClintok and her son, Robert, were carrying in platters and bowls of steaming roast beef in gravy, mashed potatoes, creamed peas, and baskets with biscuits and fresh bread, hot and crusty.

"Oh, I did, Aunt Murdoch! I danced every dance! I had two glasses of champagne, and everyone loved my new dress!"

"Two glasses of champagne? Maybe I need to attend the next one with you," Muireall said and looked at Alexander. "Does your mother know that the young women are having spirits?"

"Good Lord, Muireall! The glasses were very small, and Annabelle had some too!" Kirsty said.

"Mrs. Pendergast," Elspeth said as she glanced at her husband with a smile, "who has invited me to call her Mother, keeps a very close eye on Annabelle and Kirsty. If there was any hint of impropriety or if a young man was too forward, she or Aunt Isadora would be sure to intervene."

"So Mrs. Pendergast has invited you to call her Mother?" Aunt Murdoch asked and glanced at Muireall.

"It would hardly be fitting for you to address anyone else as Mother, Elspeth. Our mother is dead, buried at sea, if you don't remember," Muireall said as she scooped peas onto her plate.

"As if I could forget that day." Elspeth glared at her sister.

"Stuff it, Muireall," James said. "There was no disrespect meant by Mrs. Pendergast or by Elspeth. You're being a prig."

Muireall shrugged. "It is how memories are eroded. I prefer to keep those precious memories alive."

"James is right. You are being a prig. As if anything could make any of us forget our parents. She was merely trying to make me feel part of the Pendergast family, and I do feel very comfortable with Alexander's family, but I would never, ever exclude Mother and Father from my thoughts, my prayers, or my memories, or mean to replace them in any way," Elspeth said.

James winked at his middle sister. She'd never been the talkative one of the family, always preferring to stay in the background, but since her kidnapping and then her marriage to Alexander, it seemed to James that she was more confident than ever before, more willing to share her opinions. She smiled at him and then looked at Alexander, who picked up her hand and kissed her knuckles, making her cheeks redden. She was so clearly in love with him, and he with her, and to think that there had not seemed to be anything remotely similar between the two of them when they first became acquainted.

He had to look away. He didn't want any part of this romantic web that seemed to be surrounding him lately, first with Elspeth and then MacAvoy and Mrs. Emory.

"When is your next match, James?" Alexander asked.

"I want to go to it, Robert and I both," Payden said. "If we're old enough to hold a gun, then we're old enough to go see you box."

"The crowds at these matches are very rough sort of men," Muireall said. "Not company you need to keep."

"She's being a prig again, James," Payden said.

"Watch your mouth, boy. You're not too old for me to smack your behind for speaking to your sister in such a way. But if your studies are caught up and all the work is done with the canning, Alexander and his father have agreed to take you and Robert—if his mother allows," James said.

Payden let out a cheer and shoved away from the table. "May I be excused to tell Robert? I'll be right back to my seat. May I?"

Muireall glanced at James and then proceeded to eat. "You're excused."

"Who is your next opponent?" Alexander asked.

"Charley Crankshaw."

"Do you know much about him?"

"No, I don't, I'm sorry to say. MacAvoy and I were to discuss him last night, but he was late, on account of his *courting* Mrs. Emory," James said and shook his head.

"He's serious about her, James. You should not make light of him, and little Mary adores him. I would not be surprised if there was an announcement forthcoming," Elspeth said.

"MacAvoy and Mrs. Emory, you say?" Muireall asked. "Your housekeeper?"

"Who are his people, James? You were never able to say, and he's around all the time. I want to know who his people are," Aunt Murdoch said as everyone began to talk at once.

James looked at Alexander and winked. The other man chuckled into his napkin as the table erupted into three different conversations, each louder than the last. The room quieted finally, and Payden stood to help Robert clear the dishes. Mrs. McClintok carried in the warm custard topped with mixed berries they'd jarred themselves this past summer. This was the last meal he'd eat like this for a while, unfortunately. He needed to drop a few pounds before the Crankshaw fight and would have to forgo Mrs. McClintok's big meals and desserts to do it.

"Have you received your invitations to Aunt Isadora and Uncle Nathan's ball? I believe you should all be getting them," Alexander said.

"Ugh," Payden said. "I'm staying home."

Kirsty clapped her hands. "How exciting! This will be my third—no, my fourth party that I've been invited to, not even counting your wedding, Elspeth!"

"I'm so looking forward to it." Elspeth grinned. "I want to introduce you to Alexander's cousins, Benjamin and Ralph. They are very nice young men and are both home from college for the holiday."

"College men?" James winked at Kirsty. "Well, well!"

Kirsty blushed from her forehead to her chin. "Oh no. I'm not clever enough to talk to men that go to college. Maybe it's best I don't meet them. I won't know what to say."

"You are every bit as worthy as the next woman. You are bright and beautiful and loving—"

"And loud," Payden interrupted, making James and Alexander avoid looking at each other.

"And kind," Elspeth finished.

"My cousins are well-mannered young men and have been raised to be respectful of ladies. My Aunt Isadora would have had their hides if they weren't," Alexander said. "I'm certain they will enjoy meeting you."

"Oh. Oh, Alexander," Kirsty said, holding her hands to her cheeks. "You always make me feel better."

"My husband is charming," Elspeth said and ducked her head.

Alexander was a good man. Elspeth had married well, and not because he was wealthy and from a powerful and influential family. He was singularly focused on Elspeth's happiness, and nothing made his sister more content than seeing her family safe and happy. James looked between the two of them, now smiling at each other. There was love in the world. There was devotion like his parents had known. But why would he bind himself to one woman? He was far too pleased spending his time with lots of different women.

* * *

LUCINDA WAS FURIOUS. BY THE TIME SHE REACHED HER SUITE of rooms overlooking the gardens at the back of their mansion, she was seething, and she was not sure who she was angrier with, her father or the street fighter. How dare he insinuate that she was somehow bound to him! That he had gained her affections! What idiocy! He was nothing to her, even if visions of their dance had kept her awake long into the night, the feel of his hand at her waist making her flop from one side of the mattress to the other.

"Miss Lucinda?" her maid, Giselle, queried from the doorway of her dressing room. "Would you like any particular dress laid out for your luncheon?"

She had almost forgotten that she'd committed to visiting with Edith Fairchild for a meal and perhaps some shopping. She turned a calm face toward her maid. "Lay out the lavender silk and tell Mr. Laurent to have the carriage to ready at eleven." Perhaps an outing would ease her anger and divert her thoughts.

"Oh, your dress is delightful! How stylish you always are! You outshine your old friend in every way," Edith said a few hours later as the Fairchild butler took Lucinda's coat.

"How silly you are being," Lucinda said quickly, the conversation having been repeated nearly every time they met. "You know you are the most beautiful debutante Philadelphia has ever seen."

Edith shrugged, looking as if the compliment were her due, and smiled coyly. "You are too sweet," she said, pursing her lips near each of Lucinda's cheeks and wrapping her fingers around her arm. "Now come, dearest. We will have a lovely meal and maybe venture out to the shops. I am in desperate need of a new hat."

She joined Edith in a small dining room with a table placed near large windows, now letting in a weak winter sun. But it was warm and comfortable from the blaze in the massive marble fireplace nearby. The table was set with starched white linen, crystal, and silver. Lucinda listened to her friend with half an ear as the servant shook out her napkin and filled the cut-crystal glass with lemonade.

"That miserable girl, I hate her, I just hate her!" Edith said. "For her to say what she said! It's dastardly!"

"Oh no," Lucinda said, having no idea who her friend was talking about. But she would if Edith held true to form.

"Miss Mary Hershey is the devil! She was flirting with Mr. Kingley at the museum opening, batting her lashes, laughing at everything he said, practically rubbing herself on him. He was ignoring her, of course, as I was across the room from him and could see everything that happened."

"Oh dear! Right in front of you!" Lucinda said and looked up from her meal.

"And then later she was talking to some people very near me and said that Mr. Kingley would be meeting her at the park for a walk as soon as the weather was fair. She spoke loudly enough that I could hear everything!"

"I'm so sorry, Edith. I know you were coming to like him."

Edith tilted her head, holding a bite of salmon on her fork halfway to her mouth. "Like him?"

"Yes. Mr. Kingley. You said the last time we met that—"

"I don't like him any more or any less than I do anyone I am considering."

"Oh. Then you are not upset?"

"Yes, I'm upset! I'm upset at that witch, Mary Hershey. Let us make plans as to how I shall put her in her place. One would think that shocking red hair would be enough to keep her apart from our crowd, but she insinuates herself all of the time!" Edith leaned over the table. "What do you think if I start a rumor that she was being overly friendly with Simon Wurtzburg? Maybe she'd been seen kissing him, or even more!"

Lucinda stared at her friend. She could easily imagine her dropping hints about just such a rumor. In the short time they'd known each other, Lucinda had learned that Edith was very good at feigning sincerity and adding a dollop of pity while undermining a young woman's reputation. And what else did a woman have other than her reputation? Was Lucinda as shallow as Edith? As mean-spirited? There was no doubt that if she displeased Edith, she would be targeted just the same.

When she and her aunt had begun to venture into Philadelphia society, Lucinda had been flattered that well-known socialite Edith Fairchild had endeavored to meet her and include her in her crowd of friends. But sometimes the gossip and inuendo and jealousy that typified that crowd—her circle of acquaintances now as well—made her want to hole up in her suite and not venture out to meet them ever again. There was only so much spitefulness and sly, demeaning words a woman could condone or ignore. Wouldn't it be refreshing to hear some plain speaking? Or to converse with someone who was completely honest?

Like Mr. James Thompson.

Damn him to everlasting Hades for invading her thoughts. For picturing those broad shoulders, green eyes, and that chipped tooth that made her want to run her tongue over her own teeth. Edith was still plotting when dessert arrived.

"You know, if Mr. Kingley is interested in you, he will separate himself from Miss Hershey, and if he doesn't, you don't really want him anyway, do you?"

Edith stared at her. "That is hardly the point, though, is it? Mary Hershey must be made to understand who sets the rules and why it is in her best interest to follow them."

Lucinda smiled. "Of course," she said and was rewarded with a grin from her friend and hopefully an end to a conversation that was suddenly disturbing. "Where will we shop for bonnets today?"

"If my gown is ready at Fulbright's, we could shop there. I think their hat collection is excellent."

"A new gown?"

"I wanted something very special for the Pendergast ball. The sons of the family are college men and will have college brothers attend, I imagine. My mother said that would be a fine family to align with, even though their nephew, Alexander, married some loose woman from a disreputable family. His parents must be furious. I heard the bride and groom snuck away before they could be stopped," Edith said and rose from her seat. "I know the sister, Annabelle. Her prospects will diminish because of it, even with wealthy parents and a pretty face."

Lucinda had not realized that Edith was well acquainted with the Pendergast family or that she'd received an invitation. As she had understood it, her and her aunt's invitation to the ball had come because Aunt Louisa was interested in serving on the Philadelphia Hospital committee with Mrs. Pendergast. Lucinda was surprised that Edith had not heard about the dance she'd shared Elspeth Pendergast's brother since she knew the family well enough to be invited to Nathan and Isadora Pendergast's ball. But it was only a matter of time until she did hear.

Edith kept up a tirade most of the afternoon while they shopped, and Lucinda had never been so glad to see the portico of her home and Laurent waiting by the door. She climbed the steps to her rooms thinking over the day and wondered how long it would be until someone mentioned Thompson's comments to Edith. Would she then be the subject of hideous and unfair gossip? She imagined that she would be. She looked up as she neared her door to see her aunt speaking to her from only a few feet away. She'd been lost in her thoughts and had not even heard her approach.

"Lucinda, dear, how was your afternoon?"

She stared at her aunt—her mother, to be perfectly honest, as she had no recollection of the woman who birthed her. She was tired and out of sorts and wondering where she would fit in, if she ever would.

Aunt Louisa cocked her head and then opened the door to her rooms. "Come sit down. I think some tea would do you good. Or would you prefer to be alone?"

"No, I don't think so. I'll ask Giselle to get us a tray." She found her maid in the dressing room attached to her bathing room.

She came back to her sitting room, where Aunt Louisa had made herself comfortable near the fire. Lucinda seated herself, toed off her slippers, and pulled her feet beside her on the chintz-covered chair. They waited quietly until the tea arrived and Louisa could pour them both a cup. She turned to her niece.

"How is Edith?"

She shrugged. "The same, although perhaps I am different today."

"In what way?"

"She is plotting to start a rumor about a woman she doesn't like," Lucinda said. "She can be cruel."

Aunt Louisa stared at her and then focused on the fire. "I grew up with a young woman whom I thought was my dearest friend. When Renaldo began showing an interest in me, I was thrilled and flattered. He was very handsome and from a wealthy family. I dreamt of marriage to him. When it appeared Renaldo was going to speak to my papa, this friend managed to steal away with him, and they were set to be married shortly after. I don't know if he was never interested in me or if she'd tricked him somehow, but it was right at the time that we heard that your mother had died. My mother thought I would be happy if I had a change of scenery and suggested I come to America and care for you until your papa remarried. And so, here I am."

Her aunt had never shared that story with her before, and it was clear that there was still some pain for her from the memory. "Were they happy? Renaldo and your friend?"

Aunt Louisa smiled. "They did not marry. My friend was caught in a compromising position with another young man and married him. Renaldo married a few months later."

"That is sad, Aunt. There was no reason you couldn't have married, was there? And instead you were sent here to be a nurse-maid to your niece and tolerate your brother, who can be high-handed and opinionated."

Aunt Louisa stood and knelt before her, clutching Lucinda's fingers. "I've had no greater honor in my life than the opportunity to raise you, dear. From the moment your papa opened the door to the nursery and I saw you, I loved you. I will never, ever regret anything to do with my great fortune in being part of your life."

"I love you, Aunt." Lucinda watched her rise and be seated again and then stare intently into the fire as if she were across an ocean. "Have you ever heard anything about Renaldo? Is he still alive? Is there anyone still in Spain that you could ask?"

"He's very much alive," she said finally. "There is a woman, the daughter of a close friend of my mother's. She and I have corre-sponded occasionally."

"What does she say of Renaldo?"

"His wife died a few years ago, and he made inquiries to this family friend about me."

"Did he?" Lucinda smiled.

"We've been corresponding for nearly a year now. He insists he is coming to America. One of his daughters is already here and living in Boston."

"Oh, Aunt! How exciting! Will I be able to meet him?"

"I've told him to continue to Boston, that there is nothing here for him in Philadelphia."

"But why? Aren't you curious about him? About his life?"

Aunt Louisa huffed a breath and spoke sharply. "What could I possible mean to him now?" She pulled a lace handkerchief from her pocket. "I'm nothing but an old woman, past her prime, and he is undoubtedly as handsome as he ever was. You know men look wonderful with a few lines on their skin and a bit of gray at their temples." She clutched her hankie to her lips and leaned back in her chair.

"You must not think of yourself that way. You are so beautiful."

Aunt shook her head and then smiled at Lucinda. "The reason I told you that old, sad story is so you could think about Edith Fairchild in a different light. She is not a person with your interest in mind. She will always, always be thinking of herself in everything she says and does."

CHAPTER 4

James hefted a crate of jars onto his shoulder and went down the four outside stone steps that led to the kitchen and storerooms the family used for their canning business. There was no canning this time of year, but there were supply deliveries that James and Muireall arranged to receive when the stoves were cold.

"Does this all come inside?" he heard from behind him. MacAvoy was at the wagon, picking up a crate.

"Yes. It all comes down here," James called. He hadn't seen his friend for nearly two weeks, and his next fight was only four days away. The two men spent the next few minutes hauling boxes and crates inside while an impatient driver nagged at them to hurry.

"Colder than a witch's tit out here, boys. Hurry up, so I can find my own hearth and get this poor pony in clean straw," the driver shouted.

James pushed the heavy wooden door shut on the frigid air behind MacAvoy as he carried in the last box. He rubbed his hands together to warm them and glanced at his friend.

"Have you been sparring at all?" MacAvoy asked.

"Some," James said. "My corner man is mad at me, so I didn't always have a good partner."

MacAvoy rumbled a laugh. "I heard ya nearly killed poor Billy Pettigrew. What were you thinking?"

"I went easy on him. Ended up teaching him how to keep his chin down. I would have broken the kid's jaw three times if I hadn't pulled my punches."

"Are you ready for Friday?"

James nodded. "What did you find out about him?"

MacAvoy slouched on a stool. "He's a leftie. His last manager told me he likes his whiskey. But he's won pretty steadily, so he's got to be decent in the ring. New York ain't Philadelphia, but still, there's plenty of fighters there, and he's beat most of them."

"We'll find out Friday whether he's decent or not, I suppose," James said and then looked at MacAvoy. "I owe you more of an apology than I gave you before. I didn't have any reason to speculate on Mrs. Emory's virtue or intentions. I'll always treat her with the respect she deserves. It came as a shock to me, though. You've stepped out with more women than I can count, but this one you want to marry. Doesn't make sense."

MacAvoy grinned boyishly. "That's 'cause you haven't met the right girl, brother. When you do, you'll know. I feel like a babe could knock me off my feet every time I see her or that darling girl of hers. Eleanor is so beautiful, too pretty for me."

James shrugged. "She's a good-looking woman. But you've spent time with plenty of other beautiful women. Why this one?"

"They're not Eleanor, that's why. It's not just that I want to, you know, bed her, because I do. I lay awake at night and think . . . never mind."

James laughed. "I know what you're thinking about, Malcolm." He watched in astonishment as the man blushed from his hair to his chin. "My God! You're red in the face like this is the first time we ever talked about fucking."

"Well, it's not just that with my Eleanor. She's so clever! How she gets all the things done that she's responsible for at Alexander's, I'll never understand. And she's so kind and such a good mother! I just can't believe she wants to have anything to do with a knockabout like myself. She could have anyone. But she picked me." He looked up from his musings.

"You asked her, then?"

MacAvoy nodded, and for a brief uncomfortable moment, James thought he might start to cry. "She said yes, James. She's going to marry me. I'm the luckiest man in the world."

James pulled his friend to his feet and gave him a quick hug. "We're going to have to celebrate. Did Mrs. Emory set a date?"

"Spring, she said. I've got to find a house near Alexander's, but not too near as I'd never be able to afford one of those mansions. But she is set on staying as the housekeeper, if Elspeth and Alexander would allow her to live somewhere else." He cleared his throat. "Unless, of course, she was with, you know, had a baby."

James laughed at his friend's discomfort. "That could happen after you actually do some of the things you've been dreaming about at night."

"My God," MacAvoy whispered. "I could have a family. My very own family."

James squeezed his friend's shoulder. He'd met him shortly after he'd arrived with his family from Scotland at age eleven, and they'd been inseparable ever since. MacAvoy had never known his father; his mother scraped by doing piecework at one of the mills and spent her money on gin. She died when they were fifteen, and James had thought good riddance at the time, but maturity made him realize he would have taken any version of his mother in his life, whether a drunkard or not. Muireall had doled out the coin for the woman's funeral, and MacAvoy lived with them for nearly a year until he got a job that paid him enough to get a room of his own over a tavern.

"Sometimes the strangest things happen when we least expect them. Do you remember the night we met her, James? That night we got in a bit of trouble with those thugs after Elspeth? She cleaned our cuts up and fed us? From that night on, I couldn't get her off my mind. I'd try and concentrate on what the boss was saying or if you were getting your ass handed to you in the ring, and still all I could think about was her." He turned to look at James. "It will be like that for you too. Just wait."

It was on the tip of his tongue to deny what MacAvoy said, that someday he'd be hard-pressed to think straight because of a woman. But he didn't. He didn't admit to himself that Lucinda Vermeal's face flashed in his mind at the oddest moments. If he did, it would confirm his fear that he was in danger of becoming obsessed with the woman. But he'd never be interested in a snob like her, thinking herself *so* much better than anyone else. Better than *him*, was what he meant. It grated on him, her superior attitude toward him. He'd like to take her down a peg or two, but every time he thought that, he could only see himself looming over her, holding both of those delicate wrists of hers in one hand and capturing her mouth with his.

James looked up when he heard MacAvoy open the door.

"See you on Friday. Beat the tar out of Crankshaw. I need my share of the prize money."

* * *

JAMES WAS SITTING ON A HIGH PADDED BENCH, HIS BREATHING still rapid and shallow, naked other than his short drawers, a length of toweling around his neck soaking up the sweat running out of his hair, while MacAvoy looked at the cut above his eye.

"Don't think we're going to have to wake Aunt Murdoch," he said just as the door to his dressing room opened and Payden and Robert came flying in.

"Slow down, you two," Alexander said from behind them. "Give the man some room to breathe."

They'd attended tonight's match with Alexander, his father, and the man James met at the Pendergast party, John Williams. James smiled, took another drink of the water MacAvoy had handed him, and rinsed his mouth, spitting the blood into a bucket. Payden was shadow boxing in the light of the lamp MacAvoy was holding to examine James's face.

"You're going to have a blackened eye, though. What will all the women say when they see you?"

Alexander's father, Andrew Pendergast, laughed. "I imagine the ladies will think that only adds to his attraction. Congratulations. Another commanding bout."

"It was something to see," John Williams said and shook his head. "I never saw a man move his hands as fast as you did. Thank you for the ticket."

James glanced at him. "I hope you placed a bet."

"I did." Williams smiled.

"You smell, James," Payden said.

The men laughed, and Alexander ruffled Payden's hair. "Come on, boys. I promised I'd have you both home as soon as the match was over."

"Tell Muireall I won't be long and that I won't be needing Aunt Murdoch to stitch me up. I want a long soak in a tub and my bed."

"You should be glad you don't need any stitches," Alexander said. "Aunt isn't the gentlest of women with an injured man."

James laughed, making him hold his side where Crankshaw had gotten in one of his best punches. "There's no tender mercies from Aunt Murdoch, that be certain."

"I've been there when she's stitched him. Instead of trying to make a man forget that she's drawing thread through his skin, she talks about her needle likes she's tatting a pillow. Makes me near sick to my stomach," MacAvoy said.

"I heard congratulations are in order, MacAvoy," Andrew said. "Mrs. Emory is a lovely woman, worthy of a chance to start over."

"Elspeth and I have a suggestion for your living arrangements," Alexander said. "Stop and see me the next time you are visiting."

"I will, sir," MacAvoy said. "And thank you, Mr. Pendergast. I mean to make her a good husband, and I hope my work at the mill has been up to your expectations."

Alexander's father slapped MacAvoy on the back. "You're doing fine, son. We've got plans for you in a few years. Just keep at your work the way you've been doing."

"Did you hear that, James? Mr. Pendergast has plans for me," MacAvoy said when the men had corralled the boys and left the changing room.

"You're deserving of it, brother." James pulled on his clothes, only wincing once. "Let's go get our money."

* * *

"You are looking particularly lovely, Lucinda," Aunt Louisa said when she came into her dressing room as Giselle was putting the final touches on her hair.

"You look very nice too, Aunt."

"Your father wants to see us before we leave."

Lucinda looked in the mirror as Giselle dabbed rose water on her neck and wrists. "I'm sure he wants to tell us how lovely we look. Thank you, Giselle. That will be all."

The door closed softly as the maid departed. "He is in a mood, dear. Let us go and hear his tirade and then enjoy ourselves to the fullest at the Pendergasts' ball."

Lucinda would have opened the library door without knocking, but knowing that any casual behavior only irritated her father, and she would take any advantage, even if it were to wait until Laurent opened the door for her. She was quite certain what her father was going to say. There was no need to anger him further.

"Good evening, Papa. Aunt Louisa said you wished to speak to us before we left?"

Henri Vermeal stood at their entrance to the room and

trained his eyes on his daughter. He waited until the door had closed behind the two women. "I trust that you will conduct yourself in a manner befitting your family's place in society. And your aunt will make sure that all the proprieties are observed. I do not want to hear of you making a spectacle of yourself with that . . . that street ruffian. Am I understood?"

"Of course, Papa. I understand everything you have said," she replied. She walked to his chair and stood on her toes to kiss his cheek. "I will see you tomorrow. Sleep well."

The two women climbed into the Vermeal carriage and were seated side by side for the short ride to Nathan and Isadora Pendergast's home.

"I don't know what game you are playing, child, but your father is not a fool."

"I don't have any idea what you're talking about, Aunt." Lucinda turned to look out the window as the streetlights were beginning to shine.

But she did know what her aunt meant. She *understood* everything her father had said, but that did not necessarily mean she would *abide* by it. She intended to have a conversation with James Thompson. If he attended. If she did not lose her nerve. She would tell him exactly what she thought of him and his comments about her. Her stomach rolled over with the thought of confronting him. But she chided herself. She was not the daughter of Henri Vermeal for nothing. She would put that man, that street fighter, in his place.

* * *

JAMES LOOKED AT THE CROWD OF PEOPLE SURROUNDING HIM AT the Pendergast ball. Word had gotten out about his fight a few nights ago, and he'd been shaking hands with the men and had been the subject of some fluttering debutantes' lashes and a few direct looks from some married women, too, since he'd arrived.

He scanned the room occasionally for one woman in particular, the one who seemed to have lodged herself in his brain. He was glad she wasn't there.

There were plenty of willing women, and if his instincts were correct, especially a voluptuous brunette with plenty of curves to dig his fingers into. There were men, many of them, surrounding her, all wealthy and well-bred. He was guessing she was a widow, as there was nothing virginal about her. She conversed with them all but did not favor one over another, except for the alluring glances she was casting him. Maybe he would meet her later over drinks or in her bedroom. But when he pictured a bedroom with yards of lace at the windows allowing the moonlight to filter in onto a bed with a sturdy headboard, it wasn't the dark-haired, buxom woman who had just licked her lips in his direction, it was a willowy blond with bones as delicate as the lace his mother made in the old country.

"An introduction to James Thompson?" he heard from behind him and glanced in that direction to Alexander's Aunt Isadora.

"James?"

He turned. "Mrs. Pendergast. Thank you for inviting me this evening. Your party seems to be quite a success."

"Aunt Isadora, if you please, James. Yes, everyone who had replied with their acceptance is here and a few who hadn't!" She looked around at the crowd. "And it appears that you won your latest match just so you could hold court this evening."

"I win all my matches with your happiness in mind," he said with a wink and a grin while the men nearby chuckled.

"You flirt!" She slapped his arm with her fan. "My husband was very upset he couldn't attend with Alexander and Andrew, but he was told about every punch you threw over breakfast the following morning. It sounded gruesome."

"It was gruesome. Especially for my opponent."

"The reason I came over to see you, other than to make sure you were still in one piece, was to introduce to you Miss Edith

Fairchild. Miss Fairchild, Mr. James Thompson, my dear niece Elspeth's brother."

James had been watching the young woman—spectacularly beautiful and well of aware of that fact—the whole time he conversed with Isadora. She gazed at him boldly, though she gave a few surreptitious glances to a man at the edge of the crowd, who was glaring at her. She tilted her head coyly and held out a gloved hand.

"Oh, Mr. Thompson. How brave you are to enter a match to the death with another man!"

He kissed her hand, turned it palm up, and kissed her wrist. He smiled indulgently at her when he lifted his head. "Hardly a fight to the death, Miss Fairchild. My opponent still lives."

He turned his head to answer a question from another man. He didn't want any part of some spoiled debutante's plan to make the man now scowling at him jealous.

"The orchestra is starting up again, James. Be a dear and partner with Miss Fairchild," Isadora said.

There was no way he could graciously get himself out of that request. He turned to the young woman. "I'd be honored to dance with you, Miss Fairchild, if you are free."

"With me? How kind you are, sir!"

James led her to the dance floor and placed his hand on her waist, holding her as far from his body as he could, which made him think about a willowy blond whom he'd held closer than polite manners dictated. Miss Fairchild smiled up at him and glanced at the man still watching her from the edge of the dance floor.

LUCINDA HAD BEEN WATCHING HIM FROM BEHIND A GROUP OF matrons that included Aunt Louisa. She didn't believe he knew she was there, as one of the women wore huge yellow plumes in her hair that Lucinda had been able to stand behind and not been seen by most in the room. Aunt Louisa had looked at her strangely when she did not join her friends as the dancing started, many of whom were congregated around James Thompson, who was, in her opinion, the very epitome of conceit.

Lucinda had watched Edith approach Mrs. Pendergast and gesture to Thompson with a shrug and some tittering. She could just imagine what Edith was saying. But Thompson was not taken in by Edith, she didn't think, even as he smiled at her and kissed her gloved hand for an overly long time, earning a sharp look from Mr. Kingley at the edge of the crowd. No, Mr. Thompson was not interested in Edith. But there was a woman he was interested in.

Mrs. DeLuca. The young widow had been left piles of money by her elderly husband when he passed, Edith had told her. She was dark-haired and mysterious and had a sultry air about her that, combined with her vast wealth and abundant cleavage, had men of every age panting at her heels. She was signaling Thompson with little subtlety. Perfect, she thought to herself and went to find a willing—and bribable—servant after telling her aunt she was going to join with her friends gathered in the music room.

JAMES TURNED WHEN THERE WAS A DISCREET TOUCH TO HIS elbow and looked at the servant.

"Mr. Thompson?"

"Yes?"

The man handed him a folded note. He could smell its perfume without even bringing it to his nose—some expensive fragrance, as he had little doubt who had penned it. He turned away after thanking the man, but not before catching the eye of John Williams, who lifted one brow and grinned.

He read the note, winked at Williams, excused himself, and made his way across the room, avoiding those he knew as anticipation began to thrum in his veins. He would not allow a haughty virgin to interfere with his pleasure by lodging herself in his head while he prowled toward the door of the room and his target. She would stay right where she should. Far away from him.

James walked past the open door to the music room, where someone was playing the piano and several were singing with the tune. There were a few men in the library he passed, talking softly and seriously, about some pressing government matter, no doubt. He continued down the hallway and turned right as his instructions had said, down a quiet and dimly lit corridor to the next to last door. He looked right and left, straightened his tie, and ran a hand over his hair before turning the knob and letting himself into the room. It seemed deserted at first glance, a sitting room for the lady of the house, most likely. He turned when he realized there was someone else in the room. It was not whom he had expected.

Lucinda Vermeal slid into view from the shadows and leaned back against the closed door.

"Miss Vermeal. This is undoubtedly a situation neither of us would like to be caught in," he said. "Excuse me. I'm meeting someone and must have the wrong room. My apologies for disturbing you."

"No, Mr. Thompson. You do not have the wrong room. Mrs. DeLuca will not be joining you."

James narrowed his eyes and walked toward her. To her credit, she did not flinch or in any way alter her expression of disdain— and perhaps anger. What in the world could she have to be angry about?

"What is this about, Miss Vermeal? I do not appreciate deceptions."

She stared at him, the only hint of emotion the slight widening of her nostrils, as if she was preparing herself to face a foe.

"Please step aside," he said with less courtesy.

"I will not," she replied.

"Then it will be a long evening without refreshments or friends. I will climb out the damn window, if necessary, before your chaperone comes charging in to save you from my evil wiles and you both disparage my name."

He turned and strode toward the window, fully intending to somehow escape the room, and his captor, even if he had to shimmy down a tree to do so. His hand was on the sash to lift it when she spoke.

"Disparage *your* name! You, you pompous ass! Telling those men what you did about me and making my life uncomfortable for the sole purpose of your pleasure in bragging."

He turned to her. "What are you talking about?"

"At the Pendergast ball three weeks ago. What you said had come back to my Papa by the next morning."

"I really have no idea what you're talking about. I didn't say anything to any . . ." His words trailed away from her, as did his eyes.

"You do know what I'm talking about. I can see it in your face! You villain!"

James shook his head. "It was nothing. I said nothing that was disrespectful or would have belittled you."

"That can't be true. My Papa tells me that can't be true, and he has a well-developed web of friends who say it *is* true!"

"There's a young lady I was trying to discourage without insulting her. I had just danced with you, and the men in her crowd were asking about you, and I said you had enjoyed our dance. That's all."

"But you were trying to discourage another young lady, so you must have implied something more, and it was said you implied that you'd won my affections."

James shook his head. "It was not much of a remark. Maybe the gossips changed some of the details. I don't know. But it was never meant to be a claim on you."

"You don't understand my Papa and his expectations," she said and looked away, giving him a view of the long length of her very pale neck.

That was when it dawned on him what her father's real objections were. He walked closer to her, the subtle scent of roses reaching his nose, and she turned her head back to face him as he approached, those limpid blue eyes focused on him. She arched one brow as he stepped within a few inches of her.

"I think I know the real reason your daddy was so upset," he said softly and ran one finger from her cheek to her chin. She gazed up at him coolly, the only evidence of any nervousness or fear was the pulse fluttering at the base of her neck. "He wasn't upset you'd danced with a man you'd been introduced to; he was upset that it was me, a Scotsman, a boxer, and an uncouth ruffian."

She took an impatient breath. "Of course that upset him, but your comments afterward made him furious."

"You mean the comment I supposedly made," he whispered and laid his palm on her cheek, his thumb a hair's breadth from the corner of that remarkable mouth of hers, those wide, soft lips that he dreamt about. He leaned his head closer yet, staring at her mouth. "The comment that you were mine and others should stay away from the woman that James Thompson had . . . claimed."

Her shoulders and breasts rose and fell with her sharp breath. "Yes," she whispered. "Yes."

He did not know what she was agreeing to, but she didn't move to stop him when he closed the distance between them. He touched her lips lightly with his own, the contact sending a sharp pulse to his groin. He moved his hand to palm her chin, tilting her face just a bit and controlling what he thought was undoubtedly her first kiss. He ran his tongue across her lips, opening his mouth slowly as she opened hers. She shivered, her eyes closing in a languorous wafting of lashes. He touched his tongue to hers and felt her sharp intake of breath. He swept his tongue around the edge of her mouth and then deeper as he stepped closer to her, bringing her breasts against his chest and her lower stomach in contact with his cock, hard and ready.

She was a captivating mix of innocence and burning sexuality. And then she touched her tongue to the chip on his front tooth, a reminder to keep his hands up in the ring, and he jerked his hips toward hers, pinning her to the door and letting loose a deep growl. Her hands trailed up to his chest, and he caught both wrists, as slender and fragile as he'd imagined, in his free hand, slowly raising them until her arms were above her head against the door behind her. Her breasts were pressed against his chest tightly as he plundered her willing mouth.

It was the most erotic thing that had ever happened to him.

He stepped away from her, letting her wrists go, her arms falling slowly to her sides. She was staring at him, both of them breathing hard. She touched her mouth with shaking fingers. She must have felt it as much as he, he thought, that sense that certain things had irrevocably changed. And then she glanced down his body until her eyes landed where his trousers tented. She raised her gaze and lifted one pale brow.

He had an otherworldly feeling that the earth under his feet had shifted, that whatever he thought his future may or may not be had been tossed to the sky to land at her feet.

The voices in the hallway drew him from his mental ramblings, focusing again on what may happen if they were caught together, especially as she looked as if she'd just been thoroughly kissed and he had a raging cock-stand that would be difficult to hide. He reached past her and slowly turned the lock on the door. They both stared at the knob as the voices drew closer.

GOOD LORD! WHAT HAD SHE DONE? IF THEY WERE FOUND OUT, she did not know what would happen, and she could hear Edith's voice among others coming from the hall. The knob turned, and she heard the voices begin to move away from the door. She took a slow breath. She looked up at him, ready to ask him what they should do next, when he put his finger to his lips and shook his head. They waited in silence, neither moving an inch, for more than ten minutes according to the clock ticking on the mantel.

He reached for the door and gently turned the lock above the knob. He waited another minute or more and then motioned her to stand behind him. She did as he bid and watched him crack the door enough for him to peer out. He reached behind his back and felt for her hand, securing it in his. He opened the door wide, and she followed him into the hallway.

"Go back to the party. I'll slip down the servants' stairs," he said quietly.

"What have you two been doing behind a locked door?"

They both jumped and turned to Aunt Louisa's voice.

"Oh, you gave me a fright, Aunt!"

"Do not cross me, Lucinda," she said and took a look at James. "Mr. Thompson. You would be wise to heed my advice, which is to stay as far away from my niece as possible. Her father is wealthy, powerful, and determined. You would not fare well. I would advise you to hurry down those servants' steps right now before anyone comes upon us."

"Ma'am," he said, nodding to Aunt Louisa. "Miss Vermeal was resting as the result of a headache when I accidentally came upon her. My apologies for not leaving her side immediately. She is perfectly innocent."

Aunt Louisa shook her head at him and harrumphed. "Go!" She pointed to a well-concealed doorway.

He bowed when he turned to Lucinda, and the side of his mouth came up in a ridiculously appealing nod to their intimacies. "Miss Vermeal."

"You are never to dance with Edith Fairchild again. Good night, Mr. Thompson."

She turned and swept down the hallway, catching her aunt's

arm in hers. They approached the ballroom, and Edith Fairchild hurried to her.

"We have been worried about you, dearest! You just disappeared!"

"My head was aching, so I found an empty room and laid down and closed my eyes for a few minutes. As you can see, I have been restored to good health." Lucinda smiled at her friend, who looked at her as if she had seen too much.

Aunt Louisa kissed her cheek as if she'd not confronted her sneaking out of a room in company with a man. "I am so glad you are feeling better, dear. Now enjoy yourself—unless you'd like me to call for the carriage?"

"No, no, Aunt. I am perfectly recovered and would like to have some of that supper they have laid out in the next room. Suddenly, I am famished!"

Aunt Louisa walked to where matrons were gathered, and Lucinda turned to find Edith staring at her.

"I was told this evening that you shared a dance with Mr. Thompson lately and then we noticed he was missing from this party at the same time you were. Strange, isn't it?"

Lucinda shrugged and eyed her with a calm and regal look. "I suppose it would be if not for the fact that I was reclining in a room down the hall with my eyes closed and anyway, I hardly keep track of every gentleman I dance with. Come, Edith. I am starving."

CHAPTER 5

James rang the bell on Alexander and Elspeth's door. It was opened swiftly by Baxter, his sister's butler. His sister's butler! He thought to himself and laughed. His sister, who was coming down the hall toward him now, had a butler.

"Oh, thank you, Baxter. I shall take charge of my brother from here. Come in, James. Alexander is waiting for you," she said and linked arms with him.

"You're looking lovely, as usual, Elspeth. Married life must agree with you."

"Oh, it does, James." She smiled. "I couldn't be happier, especially . . ."

He stopped in the wide hallway as they approached his brother-in-law's study. "Especially?"

Her face colored, and her lips trembled into a smile. "I will be presenting Alexander with a son or daughter by late summer."

He felt tears prick the back of his eyes. His precious Elspeth, who they'd nearly lost eighteen months ago and who'd proven herself a fierce warrior in her own right. He loved her with all of his heart. He held her face in his palms.

"Elspeth. My sweet girl. You are glowing." He picked her up by the waist and swung her around.

"I see you told him," he heard Alexander say.

Elspeth hurried to her husband's side. "I'm so sorry! I just couldn't wait!"

He kissed her cheek and held his hand out to James. "Glad you could stop by."

"Congratulations to you too, Alexander!" James followed them into the library. "Your note sounded mysterious. What is it you wish to discuss?"

"I will send in a coffee tray so that you two can have your meeting. I'm joining Mrs. Emory in a moment to discuss some renovations I have planned for the bedrooms."

James watched her walk out after smiling shyly at her husband as if they had just met. He turned to his brother-in-law. "I was worried for her the last few years before her marriage. She seemed directionless and discontented. Then I was terrified for her when she was kidnapped. As proud as I was of her, she could have spent years being fearful and feeling guilty, but she has not. She has embraced her new life. You have my undying respect for caring for her and making her happy."

Alexander looked embarrassed by the praise. "I love her. I love her more than I could ever conceive of loving anyone. She is the center of my world. I would do anything to make her comfortable and happy, including," he said with laugh, "not admonishing her for scrubbing walls with the maids or sorting sheets in the laundry room. She claims that feeling useful makes her very happy. Perhaps that will stop when we have a child."

James tilted his head. "Do you think so?"

Alexander shook his head. "No," he said with a laugh. "She won't change, and that is fine with me."

"So what about this strangely worded note you sent me?"

A maid arrived with coffee and cakes, and James gladly downed a few. He needed to keep his weight up until the next fight, and all his workouts had made him drop a few pounds. He leaned back in his chair and stared at Alexander.

"I've a proposal for you via my father and uncle. They thought it might be best received from me rather than two old men," Alexander said with a chuckle. "And I agreed."

"A proposal?"

"Yes. A proposal. I'm sure you've thought ahead to the time when you are no longer able or no longer want to box to make your living. I also know you have a stake in your family's canning business and don't really know if the income from that would be enough to start a family someday."

James was staring at him, listening, but he was unable to get past Alexander saying that someday he would no longer be able to box. That comment had stopped him dead in his tracks. What could he possibly mean by that? Why would he ever give up boxing? He loved it, and it paid him handsomely.

"The idea is to build a modern gymnasium for boxers to train and to hold matches with permanent rings. To have large seating areas and comfortable dressing rooms and training rooms with their own rings. Maybe even have other events in the main area, such as musicals or shows."

"I'm not sure I understand," James said, quelling the rapid beat of his heart.

"They want you to run it, use your name in the boxing world, from New York to the Carolinas, to build a modern, profitable business. They would put the seed money in to start it but allow you, and maybe a few others, to purchase it from them over time."

James was flummoxed. Why would he want to quit boxing? Start a family? He was only twenty-five—hardly an old man. His future was his family, boxing, and willing women. Why would he ever stop?

But it occurred to him that it seemed like yesterday he was twenty and green behind the ears. Would five years seem that same short bit of time when he was thirty or thirty-five? And where would his family be then? In ten years, Kirsty would be married with children on the way, Aunt Murdoch could be bedridden for all he knew, and MacAvoy was already making his own family, much like Elspeth. Other than Muireall, his sisters and brothers would have their own lives. Would he just be the aging uncle, not quite right in the head from the number of years he'd been in a boxing ring?

He realized he'd been silent for some time.

"Just think about it, James. Maybe in a few years, you would be interested," Alexander said smoothly and shuffled some papers on his desk. "When's the next match I can look forward to?"

"I . . . I'm not sure of the date. I'll have to ask MacAvoy. He always keeps those things straight," he said and stood. "MacAvoy said he'd be here seeing Mrs. Emory if he was done at the mill in time. I'll check with him and let you know."

James walked out of the room and out a servant's door to where there was abundant air to catch his breath.

* * *

"WHAT IS IT, GISELLE?" LUCINDA SAID AS SHE FINISHED writing a letter to a friend in Virginia.

"There is a man, a gentleman, in the foyer, and he is causing a disturbance."

"A disturbance?"

"Yes. He is saying he will not leave, and he is raising his voice to Mr. Laurent, who has told him he must have an appointment to meet with the family."

"Thank you, Giselle."

Lucinda waited until the maid had gone from the room. Her father was at his club with business associates, and Aunt Louisa had come into her rooms a short while ago, a crumpled letter in one hand and a lace handkerchief in the other, saying she was going to lie down and did not want to be disturbed. She would not bother her aunt with this as, although she had been dry eyed, she'd looked quite upset and Lucinda wondered who had written the letter.

Lucinda made her way to the wide marble foyer and saw Laurent talking to a man—a tall, slender, and handsome man—while two of the family's burlier servants stood by the butler's side.

"I will march past you and open every door on the family wing if you do not fetch her immediately."

"Laurent?"

"Ah," the man said. "You must be the niece. Miss Lucinda?"

"Please refrain from shouting at our butler. It is his job to guard our family. You have me at a disadvantage, sir. Who are you, and what business do you have here?" she asked.

But he did not reply. He was looking over her head to where Aunt Louisa was coming slowly down the steps.

"Mi querida," he said softly. He went to where Louisa stood in the foyer and bent down on one knee.

"Do you know this man, Aunt Louisa?" she asked, and her aunt nodded, her gaze at some point over all of their heads.

"What are you doing here?" she asked him.

"Won't you look at me, my darling?"

The man stood slowly, taking her cheeks in his palms, bringing her face in line with his. The look of longing on Aunt Louisa's face was an intimacy that made Lucinda want to look away, but she didn't. She couldn't. He kissed her slowly then, Aunt's arms and shoulders dropping.

Lucinda turned to Laurent, as she had no intention of allowing the only mother she'd ever known to be embarrassed in front of her or the staff. "Please get everyone back to work and have a tea tray delivered to the yellow salon."

"Yes, Miss Lucinda. Right away," Laurent said, and soon the

foyer was empty other than Louisa, Lucinda, and the man now kissing her aunt's knuckles.

"Should we adjoin to a sitting room, Aunt?"

"Oh, oh yes," Aunt Louisa said, color flooding her face. "Yes. Please."

"Would you care for some tea, sir?" Lucinda asked.

"Yes. And perhaps something a little stronger," he said and smiled, following her down the hall, Aunt's hand tucked over his arm.

The tea tray arrived as they were seated, and Laurent asked the gentleman his preference and soon returned with spirits in a crystal tumbler. Lucinda and her aunt were seated side by side on the sofa, and she poured the tea since her aunt's hands were shaking so much she would have never been able to do it without spilling some in every saucer.

"Lucinda?" Aunt said and stopped to take a breath, her eyes closing as if in disbelief. "May I present Mr. Renaldo Delgado. Mr. Delgado, my niece, Miss Lucinda Vermeal."

Mr. Delgado bowed over her hand. "How do you do, Miss Vermeal?"

"Well, thank you, sir. Won't you please have a seat?" He settled in the chair directly opposite them.

"I was so sorry to hear of your wife's passing," Aunt Louisa said finally.

Delgado sat back in his seat and stared into the tumbler in his hand. "Thank you. Ann was British, you know. Her father was a diplomat, and after you left Spain, my parents arranged a marriage between the two of us; I think because they were concerned I was too depressed. And I was depressed. I didn't believe there would be any joy in my life again and did not object to the match." He looked up at Louisa. "Ann was not a happy person, not before our engagement and wedding, and not after our marriage either. But I was determined to be kind and faithful to her, and I owe her my respect as the mother of my children."

"How many children do you have, Mr. Delgado?" Lucinda asked.

"Three. Millicent, only nineteen, recently married after the year of mourning had passed. She is very young, but I believe she loves Edward and that he loves her." He looked at Louisa. "I don't believe it is right to separate young lovers. It can have disastrous consequences. My two youngest are at my hotel with the governess. Geoffrey is sixteen and Susannah is twelve."

"I'm sure they are saddened by their mother's passing," Lucinda said.

"They are. But Ann was not terribly involved in their daily lives. She was . . . ill and spent most of her time abed with her maid for company since Susannah was born. The children were with me mostly, even going to my place of business occasionally, and that has not changed. We breakfasted together every day, well, not Millicent after her marriage, of course. The four of us dined together each evening unless there was a social event I could not refuse. I tried to plan an outing with them a few times a month, to a concert or museum. Geoffrey is away at school much of the time now. I'd kept him home with tutors long after his friends were off at preparatory school, but it was time for him to begin to prepare for university. Susannah is still at home year-round and has a tutor and a governess for her education. We are all very close and hear weekly from Millicent by letter."

Lucinda smiled at Mr. Delgado. He was obviously very proud of his children and had great affection for them. She glanced at her aunt, who had tears welling in her eyes.

"I would have loved to have had your children, Renaldo. I dreamt of it," Aunt Louisa whispered, her lips trembling.

Lucinda rose and went to the door. Their conversation would become too intimate, too private for her to remain. She glanced back at them as she closed the door. Mr. Delgado was on the floor before Aunt Louisa, his head in her lap, quietly weeping. Aunt Louisa stroked his hair and gazed at him.

Lucinda climbed the stairs slowly. Finally in her suite, she pulled a worn, soft shawl around her shoulders and sat down in the tufted chair by the fireplace. Was it possible that Aunt Louisa could let go of the past and find a future with this man who clearly loved her? Their relationship could not be an idolized version of each other from their youth, but must be real, with all the hurts of their past put aside. Was twenty years too long apart?

Lucinda did not want to waste her life if she knew there was a soul that matched hers, even if it made her father unhappy, though she loved him dearly. What if James Thompson was that match? The memory of their kiss was enough to make her breasts tingle and the area below her waist throb. She blushed, remembering she'd told him he was never to dance with Edith again after he'd looked at her and winked over their intimacies. She could not understand her fit of jealousy, as there was really no other word to describe how she felt at the idea of him touching any other woman. What must he think of her? Perhaps she should get to know him a little better and ask him.

* * *

"Let's call it a day," MacAvoy shouted from outside the makeshift ring. "That's enough, Nicholson. I've got your cash here, and we'll need you back next week."

James lifted his head from the filthy wooden boards he was sprawled on, the wood shavings at his nose reeking of sweat and other smells he didn't care to think about. It took him a moment to realize he was on the floor or even where he was: a training session for his next bout. MacAvoy caught him under his arms and picked him up.

"Get your feet under you, James," he said.

He rolled his neck and shook his head, sweat flying from the ends of his hair. "Where's Nicholson? Let's go again."

"You're not going anywhere except home, boyo," MacAvoy said and led him to the small changing room.

James plopped down on the bench in the room and let MacAvoy look at the cut on his cheek. He handed James a wet rag, wrung out.

"Here. Wipe the sweat off of yourself and then get home," MacAvoy said again.

James ran the rag over his face and hair. He looked up at MacAvoy standing by the door, his hand on the latch. "What happened?"

"What happened?" MacAvoy repeated as he turned. "You got clobbered by a slow, fat bumbler. That's what happened."

"What are you mad about? I've caught a lucky punch before."

"You think that was a lucky punch? It wasn't. You were getting handled," MacAvoy's voice rose. "By Nicholson!"

"I'll get straightened out. I've got a few weeks to go."

"I'm not so sure of that."

James looked up. "You don't think I can beat Jackson? He's just a young pup!"

"Your head's not in it, James. You're distracted. What's going on?"

He looked up after several long minutes, wherein he'd hoped MacAvoy would get bored or discouraged and leave him alone. But it looked like his friend would wait him out.

"Alexander asked me to visit with him last week. I hadn't any idea why. But he proceeded to tell me some shit that his papa and uncle had cooked up about opening a real boxing arena with stands and training rooms and changing rooms. They figured that I might be considering what I'd do when I couldn't box anymore. That I'd put my name on this place, manage it, and maybe be able to buy it outright at some point. I could hardly believe it!"

"My God," MacAvoy whispered.

"I know! That's what I thought. Why would I be thinking about quitting boxing?"

MacAvoy was staring at him and shaking his head. "Don't tell me you turned him down."

James shrugged. "I didn't answer, and Alexander just changed the subject."

"What do you mean, you didn't answer? Can you still give him an answer?"

"I guess. I didn't want to insult Alexander or his family. They're so good to Elspeth and to the rest of us. He changed the subject, and I went along."

MacAvoy ran a hand down his face and dropped to his haunches, eye level with James. "You're my best friend. You were my only friend, and your family took me in when I had nowhere to go. I love you and Payden like brothers and the girls like sisters. So I'm going to talk to you, brother to brother. Go back to Alexander and tell him you're in. Tell him to tell his father that you're flattered by their interest and are ready to plan for the future."

"What are you talking about? We're not finished! At least, I'm not!"

"James!" MacAvoy grabbed his shoulders and shook. "You've only got a couple more years. That's it. You're at the top of your game now, but there'll be a boy in the not too distant future who will take you down in front of a crowd. There'll be a new king. It's just the way it is."

James was breathing hard, trying to control the wild beating of his heart. "I've got longer than a couple of years," he whispered, his voice shaking.

"Maybe you do. Maybe you don't. But if you don't plan now how and where you'll support yourself, you'll end up washed up, nobody willing to hire you except to pour ale at the Water Street Tavern. Whatever this scheme Mr. Pendergast has cooked up will take years to come full-term. By then, you may need a job." MacAvoy looked away and turned back to James with regret. "I wasn't planning on telling you this yet, but I told Graham to keep me in mind for more evening work in the future. Not right now, with you still fighting, but in the future."

James watched as MacAvoy straightened to his full height, pulled on his coat and hat, and left James sitting, his towel around his neck, his muscles tightening with the chill air seeping in around an ill-fitting window, newspaper stuffed into its sides. He was going to walk the long way home.

* * *

LUCINDA WAS STILL IN THE TUFTED CHAIR BEFORE THE FIRE when there was a knock at her door. Her aunt came in the room, looking nervous and restless.

"Come sit down, Aunt Louisa. I'd call for a tray, but it will be dinner soon. Giselle has already been here trying to coax me into changing my dress, but I told her to come back in a bit. I was hoping you would come see me."

"Oh, Lucinda. My head is spinning," Aunt said as she sat on the edge of the chair next to her. "Your father will be home soon."

"What will you tell him?"

"Mr. Delgado is coming back with his children to dine this evening," she said breathlessly, holding her hand to her bosom. "I don't know what to think."

Lucinda smiled. "I think you'd best get Berta to lay a cold towel on your eyes. You don't want to meet everyone looking as if you've been crying for hours, do you?"

Louisa smiled and bit her lip. "I would like to look my best. What did you think of him?"

"He's very handsome. Well-spoken and charming. But what makes him so very appealing is how much he adores his children and how very much he has been longing for you for so many, many years."

"He does love them, doesn't he?" she asked, her eyes glistening. "And he is every bit as handsome today as he was twenty years ago."

Lucinda smiled. "And he loves you. I think he always has."

Louisa took a shuddering breath. "Is it possible? Do you think he has loved me as I've loved him all these years?"

"What did he say about the woman who was your friend?"

"My father spoke to Renaldo and convinced him that I was not really interested in him," Louisa said and looked up. "I think my father was hoping that I would remain unmarried and care for him and my mother as they grew older. When I think back on everything now, it was my mother who insisted I move to America to raise you. I imagine she did not want me to become a nurse maid."

"Go now. Let Berta get you into that lovely lilac gown. You look so beautiful in it. Not that you don't always look beautiful."

Louisa stood and went to the door. "Don't worry, though, dear. I will never desert you. You are the daughter of my heart, and I would never, ever put anything over your happiness," she said without turning and quickly slipped out.

CHAPTER 6

James came up the basement stairs in the alley beside Green's Grocery. He had just completed the delivery of twelve cases of their jarred goods while Kirsty was inside the store with the owner settling the bill. It was a warm day for January, a rare treat, with no rain or snow, and he was dressed in what Muireall called his homespun: wide-leg pants over heavy leather lace-up boots, a collarless shirt, and plain vest with a loose-fitting jacket of plain brown wool over it all, for carrying their crates down alleys, into storerooms, and shelving boxes if asked. He pulled his flat cap from his head and wiped his forehead on his sleeve.

He walked to the street, busy now with shoppers out on a pleasant day, carrying bags and packages, looking for Kirsty. She came out of Green's door just then.

"Did you get it all delivered?" she asked as they turned to walk down the street toward the wagon he rented for deliveries.

He nodded. "That's the last of the orders. Let's get home. I'm hungry and need to check on Payden. Muireall said he and Robert have been getting into some trouble."

"Not really trouble, or at least pretty insignificant trouble. The old woman who moved into the house beside the Mingos told Aunt Murdoch that the two boys had walked through her yard. She was furious."

"For cutting through a neighbor's yard? MacAvoy and I did it all the time."

"That's why I don't think there is any urgency with Payden," Kirsty said. "Oh, James. Stop a moment. Let me look in this window. There are so many beautiful dresses and gloves. Look! Just look at that gold satin. I would look gorgeous in that!"

James smiled down at her and laughed. "My God, Kirsty, your vanity knows no bounds. You're going to have to marry a man who is not impressed with your beauty."

"I'm not vain," Kirsty began and grinned as James touched her elbow to move her from the door of the dressmaker to make way for two women coming out.

He could not believe who the women were.

"Mr. Thompson!" Lucinda Vermeal said with some surprise.

He doffed his hat. "Miss Vermeal. A lovely day to be out, is it not?"

"It is," she said and then hesitated, glancing at Kirsty. "Would you introduce your friend to my aunt and me?"

"Oh, Miss Vermeal!" Kirsty said. "I have seen you at several parties and have so admired your dresses and hair. I'm so happy to meet you! I'm James's sister, Kirsty Thompson!"

James smiled at his sister's enthusiasm and hoped the Vermeal ladies would not be haughty or rude to her.

"It is very nice to meet you, Miss Thompson. This is my aunt, Miss Louisa Vermeal. What brings you out today with your brother?"

"We were delivering canned goods our family makes to Green's Grocery." Kirsty pointed behind her to the storefront. "This is our last stop for the day, and I couldn't help but notice that beautiful gold dress in the window. I told my brother I would look gorgeous in it, but he said I was vain! Can you believe that?" She laughed unaffectedly.

James glanced at Miss Vermeal, who was, he was thankful, smiling at Kirsty's enthusiasm. The aunt walked over to the window beside Kirsty.

"Show me which one, Miss Thompson," she said.

"That one in the back with the netting around the neck," Kirsty said.

The aunt pointed to something else in the window, and the two of them turned their backs to him and Miss Vermeal, who was looking at him now with one raised brow. She was not smiling, but he had an overall feeling of gladness, of rightness in her company, and the spots of color on her cheeks made him think she felt the same. He realized then that he was in his delivery clothes and did not look the way she was accustomed to seeing him.

"Excuse my less than formal attire," he said. "I was the delivery boy today."

She glanced down his body, making his blood heat, taking her time until her gaze climbed back to her eyes. "As you are well aware, Mr. Thompson, there is little you could do to make yourself less appealing."

"Are you saying I am vain?" he said with a smile.

"I am saying that you are the most overly confident man I've ever met."

James thought Miss Vermeal was matching his light tone; however, her comment made him falter. Did he see himself as invincible? Too sure of his own abilities and unable to be realistic as to what the rest of his life would be like as he grew older?

"Mr. Thompson, you are looking far too serious. Your confidence is attractive. You must know that."

He shook his head and looked across the street to the small park, wishing he was alone with her and wondering why. Because he wanted to tell her about what was troubling him and wondered what she would think of Alexander's plan?

"James!" Kirsty said excitedly. "Miss Vermeal and I are going into the shop. Do you mind terribly? Maybe Miss Lucinda will stay and keep you company."

The aunt glanced at Lucinda with a smile and led Kirsty into the shop, the bell tinkling as they entered. He looked at the woman in front of him. She was the very picture of cool beauty. Her white-blond hair pulled up loosely under a small hat, sitting at an angle atop her head, and her pale skin a contrast to the dark blue of her heavy silk-lined cloak. Men—and women—glanced at her more than once as they walked past them. She was that kind of woman. The kind who stopped men in their tracks.

"Would you like to step across the street, Miss Vermeal? There's a small park, and I see a vendor selling sandwiches." She walked over to a young man standing near the building. He hadn't realized they were accompanied by a servant. She handed the young man her package and spoke to him. She turned then and raised her brows.

"Will you join me?" he said, and she fell into step beside him. "You bring a servant with you when you shop? The streets of Philadelphia during the day are generally safe for two women together, or so I thought."

"My father is very old-fashioned. He insists we bring someone with us, and not just a maid, although my aunt is my chaperone, but a young man to see to our safety. The maid is in our carriage just down the street."

"We must appear like a pair of ragtags, Kirsty and I, to you and your aunt."

"You appear to be free, Mr. Thompson; that's how you appear. You and your sister both," she said and took his arm as they navigated the uneven street and horse droppings.

"Kirsty is . . . enthusiastic. Thank you for tolerating her as she went off on her favorite subject: herself," he said with a laugh. "But she is a dear girl."

"She seems to be unencumbered by some of society's more

ridiculous rules. She seems to just be herself. That is a blessing, I think."

He guided her to an unoccupied bench and waited until she was seated. "Would you like anything? A lemonade? Roast beef?"

"A lemonade would be appreciated."

James went to the vendor across the expanse of the wide graveled path and waited his turn impatiently. Did he mean to talk to her about something serious? He finally got his sandwich, shredded beef with a slice of cheddar between two slices of dark bread wrapped in paper, and a mug of lemonade. She was watching him as he dodged other walkers and made his way to where she sat. He seated himself beside her.

"That smells delicious," she said after sipping her lemonade.

"Do you want a bite?" He held the sandwich out to her.

"What? Oh no. That would be . . ." she said, still eyeing his food. "Impolite."

"There's plenty, and I'm willing to share."

She shook her head. "That is a cardinal rule in my house. I would never be caught taking something from someone else's plate. My papa would have an apoplexy."

"Really? Then it's best you never dine with the Thompsons." He laughed and then pictured her at a Sunday dinner, seated to his left. He swallowed. "Aunt Murdoch would smack our hands, and my older sister, Muireall, would glare, but that doesn't stop the occasional, 'You were finished,' said after stabbing something off your neighbor's plate. Payden is famous for it, but then he's a growing boy. Even Kirsty, every once in a while."

She looked at him so wistfully that he wanted to take her in his arms and promise that he would make everything right for her.

"I would have to be on my guard, then," she said and looked at him directly. "If I was ever invited to dine with your family."

He nearly groaned aloud. What was it about this woman that made every one of his emotions, especially the ones tightly bottled, bubble up when he was in her company? He stared back at her and cleared his throat.

"Have a bite. Go ahead." She looked at him as if he were asking much more than what he was, but she eyed the sandwich, looked around at the passersby, and took it out of his hands. She took a small bite and closed her eyes, those long pale lashes fluttering against her cheeks.

"That is delicious," she said.

"Have another bite, if you want," he said in a low, throaty voice. She did and stared at him over the top of his sandwich. She handed it back, and he took a large bite.

"Why did you look at me like you did when I said you were overconfident?" she asked.

He swallowed. "What do you mean?"

She smiled and looked away, watching people walk by. She took the last sip of her lemonade and gathered the strings of her purse, as if preparing to stand up. She looked at him.

"Thank you, Mr. . . ."

"My brother-in-law came to me with a plan his father and a relative had for opening a boxing arena. They wanted to know if I would put my name on it and manage it, maybe even buy it in a few years."

"That sounds promising," she said and looked at his profile. He had put down his sandwich on the bench and was bent over where he sat, his elbows on his knees, his hands clasped in front of him, staring out into the crowd of people walking by. "But you are not pleased."

He did not turn his head. "They think I'm washed up. That my boxing days are done. MacAvoy thinks I'm going to end up pouring beer at a seedy tavern when I can't box anymore."

He was in a pique, she was certain, even though he'd not raised his voice or displayed any other masculine contrivance. She would have smiled at his behavior, but she did not think it was the right thing to do. "Who is 'they,' and who is MacAvoy?"

"Alexander, my sister Elspeth's husband, and his father and uncle. MacAvoy. My best friend since we moved here from Scotland. My closest friend. Used to be my closest friend. Now there's a woman telling him what to do and how to think."

She smiled then. She couldn't help it, although he was still staring straight ahead. "They told you that you were washed up?"

"No." He finally looked at her. "They didn't have to. Why else would they want me to lend my name to this thing of theirs?"

"Perhaps they thought you were very intelligent and skilled with people. You've got experience in your family's business. Maybe they see a winning horse and want to bet on him."

He swallowed visibly, and she could barely tear her eyes away from the muscles working in his neck, his skin tan and taut.

"Most people think I box because I'm too dumb to do anything other than let men punch me like a sawdust-filled bag."

She stared at him, knowing he was in pain, knowing he was unsure of himself and hurting. "I think you are—"

"James! James! You will not believe what I've bought! But of course you will believe it! What a ridiculous thing for me to say!"

James stood and smiled at his sister, nodding to Aunt Louisa behind her. "Thank you, ma'am, for accompanying her to the dressmakers. It saved me from doing so."

"Kirsty is a delight, Mr. Thompson," Aunt said. "I enjoyed her enthusiasm."

"She helped me pick out a dress for Elspeth's dinner. Oh! Oh yes! I must talk to my sister immediately and make sure you are both invited," Kirsty said hurriedly. "Come, James. Take me to Elspeth's right away. It was so wonderful meeting you both!"

Kirsty smiled at Lucinda and Aunt Louisa and tugged on her brother's arm. He shook his head and looked at her indulgently as she stood on tiptoes and kissed his cheek.

"It's been a pleasure seeing you, Miss Vermeal," he said to her aunt and then turned to her. "I enjoyed our conversation very much. Perhaps we will get a chance to finish it sometime."

She stared at him. He was purely adoring of his sister and not afraid in the least to reveal it. She could have pressed herself up against his body, right there in front of her aunt, his sister, and all the gawkers that action would elicit. There was a pull between them she'd never experienced before, and she wanted more of it. She didn't want it to end.

"Fascinating," she said. "Fascinating was what I was going to say earlier."

He smiled slowly at her, showing off that small chip on his front tooth and making her blush. "It was very nice to meet you, Miss Thompson. Aunt? We'd best be getting home."

* * *

"I HOPE THAT THIS EVENING I WILL NOT BE SUBJECTED TO THE children you insist on inviting so often, Louisa," Henri Vermeal said as they were seated for dinner several days later.

"Not this evening, no, Henri, although I believe 'subjecting' is a bit strong a word for two young people who have been delightful and intelligent, with exceptional manners," Aunt Louisa replied. "I'm meeting them tomorrow for an outing to the Philadelphia Library."

"I have no idea why you cultivate his acquaintance. He strikes me as someone of little consequence. It's no wonder that Father discouraged his suit all those years ago." He lifted one arched brow. "Twenty years? A lifetime."

Aunt laid down her fork and knife on either side of her plate and looked at her brother across the length of the table. "We have discussed marriage in general terms, and if he formally proposes to me, I will marry him once Lucinda is settled in her own marriage."

"That's preposterous! There are duties here that I need you

for, Louisa. Continue to indulge yourself if you must with outings with him and his brood, but anything more than that is out of the question."

"Is it, Henri? I am independently wealthy and well past the age that I seek or require your approval."

"Independently wealthy, are you?"

"Don't threaten me, Henri," Aunt said. "If I walked out of this house with nothing but the clothes on my back, it would not matter. Renaldo is very, very wealthy."

"I need you to attend to things here!"

"Then marry again, Henri. Leave Lucinda and me out of your schemes."

"Speaking of Lucinda," her father said and turned to look at her. "I have received invitations for us to a dinner at the Pendergasts'. This is the son of the family whose new wife is sister to that . . . that street ruffian. We will not be attending. I'll send our refusal forthwith."

"Really, Henri? I would have thought you would be delighted to attend a dinner where the host's uncle, Mr. Nathan Pendergast, and his wife, Isadora, are attending. The wife's brother sits on the board of that railway you are so interested in. But what do I know about the intricacies of business?" Aunt said.

Lucinda so enjoyed watching her aunt manage her father. He would bluster and shout and eventually quietly concede. For her part, she allowed her father to maintain his dignity and changed the subject completely.

* * *

"YES, YOU MUST GO," JAMES SAID TO PAYDEN. "THIS IS YOUR sister's first party. Just think how hurt she would be if you didn't attend."

Payden stormed out of the parlor, leaving Muireall, with her stitching, and James.

"You seem keen to attend this party," Muireall said. "I agree with Payden. I'd much rather stay home than attend another event with 'good' society."

"Elspeth would be crushed if you didn't attend," James replied, shaking out the newspaper in his hands and folding it until he was on the page listing the businesses looking for workers.

"Kirsty told me about the two women she was introduced to last week when you took the delivery to Green's," Muireall said. "She said you walked across the street with the young woman while she shopped with the woman's aunt. She also told me she is the most beautiful woman she's ever seen."

"Really?" James studied the list in the paper. "I hadn't noticed."

Muireall harrumphed. "Do you think stories of the women who you court, although none of them good enough to bring here to meet your family, don't reach my ears? You are infamous with the unmarried ladies, James, and apparently a favorite among the widows."

"You shouldn't listen to gossip."

"Except this young woman, as Kirsty described, did not seem the least intimidated by you or enthralled with your attention. She said she seemed aloof to you but was kind to her. That makes me wonder about her."

"Nothing to wonder about, Muireall. Kirsty has always got romance on her mind. She sees it everywhere."

"Elspeth has added her, her father, and her aunt to the guest list."

James shrugged. "Kirsty will be pleased. She was much in awe of Miss Vermeal."

"And you, James? Are you in awe of Miss Vermeal?"

"In awe? She's a snob, Muireall. I have no time for that," James said and buried his face in the paper.

There were several listings for laborers and carpenters. He had no idea how to be a carpenter, and he didn't particularly want to dig ditches, which was mostly what the laborers he knew did, that and haul heavy shingles, bricks, and blocks. He could always go work at the Pendergast mill, where MacAvoy worked. Alexander's father would put in a good word for him, and he supposed he could learn to run one of the massive looms his friend described. He didn't think he could work for MacAvoy; that would put too much of a strain on their friendship, especially if MacAvoy had to fire him. If these jobs were as boring and repetitive as they sounded, he would do something stupid just to liven his day. What would Lucinda Vermeal think of him if he were a laborer in a mill? He put that thought aside quickly.

"How did we do last year?" he asked.

"Do?"

"The business. The canning business. I imagine you'll be closing the books on last year soon and adding up all the columns. How did we do?" He dropped the paper to his lap and looked at his eldest sister.

"We did fine. A little better than the prior year. I'm going to invest part of it in some new labeling equipment. Why do you ask?"

"Just wondered. One of these years, I may set up in my own rooms somewhere, when Kirsty marries and Payden goes off to school."

Muireall stared at him. "You're assuming I'll live out my life here with Aunt Murdoch."

"Do you have any big plans? You never even leave the house. I assumed you'd stay here until . . . until . . ."

"Until one of my siblings buries me and sells the house?"

"Now you're being morbid."

"We cleared around two thousand dollars. I'll split it between the six of us and give Mrs. McClintok a bonus. She's saving for an education for Robbie, and she deserves it."

"I don't care if she gets some of the money. We couldn't do what we do without her. So I'll clear three hundred dollars or thereabouts," James said. He had a little nest egg of gold in a pouch buried in the wall of his room and some paper money in the bank from his fights, although sometimes he spent it without thinking, especially after a bout when he and MacAvoy were celebrating and buying rounds for everyone in the tavern, and ten dollars went to Daisy too. "The money from Mother and Father still pays for all the household expenses, or do you have to pay for things out of the canning business?"

"This house and all the expenses surrounding it, including personal items for any of us, is paid for from the interest on the monies brought from Scotland. I have the principal in a variety of investments in case there's a bank failure or some catastrophe."

"You've kept us afloat all of these years, even when we first came here and you were very young," he said, looking at Muireall with the respect she no doubt deserved.

"Aunt helped in the beginning, but she was never terribly interested. I enjoy keeping the books and keeping our family as comfortable as possible within our means." She looked up at him. "What precipitates this sudden interest?"

He thought about telling her of the offer from the Pendergasts but had some odd feeling that he wanted to keep it close to the vest. Maybe until he could understand it more fully. Maybe until he'd had a chance to finish his conversation with Lucinda Vermeal. He groaned aloud with that foolish thought.

"What was that for?" Muireall asked.

CHAPTER 7

"Thank you for inviting us," Lucinda said to Elspeth Pendergast as she stepped into the Pendergast home and handed a servant her cape.

"We are so happy that you could join us, Miss Vermeal, and your father and aunt too. Kirsty came to see me right after she'd met you and insisted we invite you."

"Mr. Vermeal? Welcome to our home," Alexander Pendergast said.

Lucinda watched her father shake hands with the host and kiss the hand of the hostess with his best superior attitude on display. It would be difficult for this young couple to not realize he was being so infuriatingly condescending and haughty. But they were both gracious and warm in their greetings. Elspeth Pendergast looked at her husband as if he set the stars in the sky, and he was no less conspicuous when he gazed at her and touched her arm.

She followed her father and aunt as they were directed down a long hallway to a set of open double doors. The room was crowded and filled with laughter and chatter.

"Dear Lord," her father said. "Can't these people speak to each other at a normal level? It's like walking into a circus."

"If you wish to go, Henri, we will make your excuses," Aunt said as Kirsty Thompson hurried to them.

"I've been waiting right there," she said with a broad smile and turned to point to a group of young people, "so that I wouldn't miss your arrival."

Aunt laughed and gestured to Kirsty's gown. "I was right. You look beautiful in that color."

"You were! I would have never guessed that it would suit, but it's perfect!" she said, swinging her skirts and then glancing at Henri Vermeal. "Oh, oh. Where are my manners? I'm sorry. My name is Kirsty Thompson; my sister is the hostess, Elspeth Pendergast."

He stared at her and her outstretched hand. "Miss Thompson," he said finally, taking her hand in his and kissing the back of it.

"Oh," Kirsty said, now red-faced. "You're so elegant!"

Lucinda held her breath. Her father was not skilled at being charming to outspoken young women. More than likely he would be dismissive, and then Aunt or she would have to cover his harsh words, whatever they may be. Her father shook his head and then smiled, actually smiled.

"Miss Thompson, I am charmed," he said. "My sister is right. You look lovely in that dress, although I imagine you look lovely in whatever you choose to wear."

Kirsty's face reddened further. "I . . . I . . ."

"I assume you know your brother-in-law's family to some degree?"

"Oh yes. The Pendergasts are very good to me and include me in their parties and outings."

"How kind of them. I would like to meet young Mr. Pendergast's aunt and uncle. We have a mutual interest, and I am anxious to make their acquaintance. Could I count on you to manage the introductions?"

"Do you mean Aunt Isadora and Uncle Nathan?"

"I believe I do," he said with a smile.

"Oh yes. Come with me, sir." She slipped her hand around Henri's arm. They walked away as Kirsty chattered on.

"Dear me," Aunt said. "I was worried he'd be short with her."

"I am amazed that he was so pleasant, especially to someone as . . . enthusiastic as Kirsty. But then, he wants an introduction to Isadora Pendergast's brother."

"At least he is out of our hands." Aunt grinned. "Let us find a servant and enjoy some champagne."

Lucinda nodded at several acquaintances as she and her aunt wandered the edge of the room, sipping their drinks and looking at the artwork and sculptures. Apparently, the Pendergasts were collectors. She turned to the door as the chatter from the crowd increased.

And there he was. James Thompson looked devastatingly attractive in his dark suit and gold vest, already surrounded by some young men and women. Her heart skipped a beat as he found her in the crowd and held her eyes with his. She turned back to her aunt, who was discussing a bust on a tall pedestal.

"Lucinda, dear," Aunt said. "Are you well? Your cheeks are bright red."

"I'm fine," she replied in a breathy voice, glancing over her shoulder at the crowd at the door. Her aunt looked that way and smiled at her.

"He is uncommonly attractive," she said after a long sigh.

"He is rather handsome," Lucinda said and stared up at a painting, her back to the door.

"Mr. Thompson, it is very good to see you again, isn't it, Lucinda, dear?" Aunt said.

She turned, preparing herself for the magnetism that seemed to crackle between them. "Mr. Thompson."

"Ma'am," he said with a nod to Aunt. He turned to her, and his eyes traveled leisurely over her, a small grin on his face. "You manage to make every other woman here dim in comparison, Miss Vermeal."

They looked at each other for a few long minutes, long enough that Aunt turned away to another piece of artwork, leaving Lucinda to drink in the sight of him, his freshly shaven cheeks, his twinkling green eyes and dark tousled hair. She desperately wanted to touch him, push back the curl of hair that was falling over his brow or touch the bump on his nose. He lost his grin as she leaned toward him, her breath coming in shallow pants.

"James!" she heard from behind him and leaned back quickly.

"MacAvoy is here, James. Did you see him? Oh. Hullo."

She smiled at the young man, who was now staring at her. He looked remarkably like James but with auburn hair. He would break some hearts in a few years.

"Miss Vermeal? My brother, Payden. Payden, this is Miss Lucinda Vermeal and her aunt, Miss Vermeal," James said.

"How do you do," she said.

"Very well." He smiled at her. "Now that I've gotten to meet the prettiest lady in the room."

"Payden," James said sharply. "Mind your manners."

"She is the prettiest lady in the room," the boy said.

"I'm well aware of that, but you don't go . . ." James took a breath. "Miss Vermeal, please excuse my younger brother's manners."

Aunt laughed. "This one will be a favorite of the ladies, I think."

"James?"

They all turned to a younger woman and an elderly one who'd just smacked James's arm with a fan.

"Misses Vermeal? This is my oldest sister, Muireall Thompson, and my aunt—actually, my Great-Aunt Murdoch. This is Miss Lucinda Vermeal and her aunt, Miss Vermeal."

. . .

James put a hand on the back of Payden's neck to keep him from staring at Lucinda Vermeal's cleavage. He was having enough trouble himself keeping his eyes on her face and not on those very, very white breasts, lounging in folds of rose-colored silk and moving with her every breath.

She and Muireall were having an interesting stare that lasted a few moments, neither woman smiling or showing any hint of welcome. Aunt Murdoch, however, had sized up the situation with a quick glance.

"Miss Vermeal?" Aunt Murdoch said to Lucinda's aunt. "Won't you take a turn around the room with me? When I'm visiting my niece Elspeth, I never have time to admire all the pictures and whatnot that she and her husband display."

"Certainly, Mrs. Murdoch."

"Payden and I have yet to speak to Elspeth's in-laws. Excuse us," Muireall said with a last long look at Lucinda. He turned back to her.

"You've met the whole clan now." He smiled at her, thinking he had her to himself for a few minutes.

"Your sister is formidable," she said.

"That's one word for her," he said. "But she is the way she is because she's had great responsibility placed on her shoulders since she was twelve years old. Someday I'll tell you that story."

"And your aunt is a schemer." She smiled wryly.

"'Tis a good description of Aunt Murdoch, and if it means I get a few minutes alone with you, then I am heartily glad she is one."

"You're a flatterer, just like that young brother of yours. He looks like you."

James gazed across the room at Payden as he was speaking to Alexander's parents. They laughed at something he said. "Hopefully, his studies will induce him to be something different than me."

"Why do you want him to be different than you?"

He glanced at her. "Because I don't want him to get paid to get his brains bashed in."

"That's just an occupation."

"Just an occupation?"

"Yes. Just an occupation. We are all more than what we do to earn our living, although women have virtually no opportunity to earn anything."

"Rich women may not. But come to my neighborhood and you'll find plenty of women who work, either in the mills or breweries or some business out of their home."

"You're very angry today," she said softly. "And I don't think it's because I come from a wealthy family."

"I'm not angry." He looked away from her.

She reached for the champagne she'd sat on a marble table earlier and walked away from him.

Damn her, he thought. She had the ability to read his moods like no one he'd ever met, other than maybe MacAvoy, but he could fool his best friend if he tried, and James had a feeling he'd never be able to fool her. And she had no patience with him when he was untruthful or changed the subject away from something he did not wish to discuss.

He looked up from his musings and found himself under the eyes of a tall, distinguished-looking man, staring at him with what could only be called malice. Then he saw the older Miss Vermeal speak to him. He did not look at her, but kept his eyes focused on James across the room. James stared back, without blinking, barely taking a breath. Lucinda's father. They would go a few rounds, he thought.

Dinner was called by the butler a short time later, and he gathered up Aunt Murdoch and the elder Miss Vermeal, who were standing together when he found them, one on either arm, and followed Payden with Muireall ahead of them to the ballroom that had been set up with several long tables to accommodate all of the guests. He took a quick look for Kirsty and saw her on the arm of a tall, thin man with spectacles. She was white-faced, staring straight ahead and saying nothing, which was a surprise on its own. He wondered who the man was.

Elspeth hurried to his side as he stepped into the ballroom.

"Aunt Murdoch, I have you over here near Alexander's great-aunt and uncle."

"Put the old tarts together, eh?"

Elspeth rolled her eyes and took Aunt Murdoch's arm to lead her away.

"It looks like we are seated side by side, Mr. Thompson," Lucinda's aunt said, looking up at him.

He did not wait for a servant to manage her chair but seated her himself and stared off a young man in uniform when he came to help James with his own chair. "I'm well able to seat myself," he said. "Go help some of the women."

The soup was served, and Miss Vermeal leaned close to him. "So tell me, Mr. Thompson, what is it about my niece that you cannot help yourself from staring at her?"

"I'm not sure what you mean, ma'am."

"Don't be coy with me, young man. I may be the only thing between you and Lucinda's father if whatever this is moves beyond flirtation."

"What could I possibly offer an accomplished and sought-after woman like Miss Vermeal?" he said, failing to keep the bitterness out of his voice.

"Oh dear." She laid her fingertips on his arm. "You are quite in love with her, aren't you?"

"How ridiculous," he said and stared at the woman beside him.

But was it ridiculous? It explained this obsession he had with her. Planning when he would see her next. Thinking about her at the odd moment during the day. Dwelling on that kiss between the two of them when he lay in bed at night, and often relieving himself of the ache he felt with his own fist as he pictured her in his mind's eye, her delicate hands above her head in his grasp and the feel of her straining toward him. He shifted in his seat.

"Lucinda clearly finds something of worth in you. I've never seen her express more than the slightest interest in any man. Of course, her father has plans to marry her off to someone of his choosing, who would manage the Vermeal holdings when he is gone."

"He would force her?"

"Lucinda is not easily manipulated, but that path may appear to be for the best, especially if she does not see any alternatives."

James turned his head to look at Lucinda's aunt, but she'd already begun a conversation with the man on her other side. That had been a warning, he supposed, that if he was interested in her—other than a quick fuck, which would never happen in any case—he'd better get organized and declare himself. He looked up to see her father focused on him. He stared back.

By the time the main course had been cleared, James was ready to pick up the bounder seated to Lucinda's left, carry him to his sister's front door, and throw him out on the street. He leaned too close and even stretched an arm along the back of her chair.

Alexander stood from his seat at the head of the main table. "Coffee, tea, spirits, and dessert will be served in the next room." Elspeth stood, looking shy and beautiful, and put her hand on her husband's arm as they led the guests through the open doors behind him.

LUCINDA WAS SO THANKFUL THAT DINNER WAS FINALLY OVER and she could remove herself from Benedict Bartholomew's reach. She slipped ahead of two older women as she made her way down the aisle between the tables, putting some distance between herself and Mr. Bartholomew's hand. She shivered, remembering how he'd stretched his arm around her chair and touched her bare back with his fingers. It was enough to make her sick. She was looking for Aunt Louisa when she felt a hand at her arm.

"Did you enjoy your dinner?" she asked James Thompson as she glanced over her shoulder to confirm what her intuition had told her. He was guiding her with light pressure at her lower back through the crowd gathering near tables with elaborate desserts and past servants handing out delicate china cups of tea and coffee. The men were mostly gathered near a servant pouring brandies and whiskeys.

He moved her through a door that servants were rushing in and out of and down a hallway. He stopped at a closed door and looked behind them.

"In here," he said and turned the knob.

The room was dimly let by a low flame in the fireplace. She wandered toward it, watching the wood crack and hearing its hiss. She turned when she felt him behind her.

"I didn't care one bit for that boy beside you with his arm around your back. Did he touch you?"

She stared into his face, his sparkling green eyes intense and blazing. "He touched my back, but I moved out of his range. I'm accustomed to handling men like that."

"I'll kill him," James said in a low, gravelly voice.

"You really needn't do that, especially now," she said and stepped an inch closer to him.

He crowded her further. "Why 'especially now'?"

"I'm here with you, aren't I? And you have your hand on my waist."

He smiled that devastating smile of his. "I do, don't I?"

She pursed her lips into a smile and laughed lightly. He stared at her mouth and closed the few inches between them. His touch was light, his eyes drowsy but focused on her. She could smell an earthy cologne and mewled when he ran his tongue over her lips.

He opened his mouth over hers, touching her tongue with his, his hand around the back of her neck, holding her still as if she was going to try and escape the magic he made.

His hand slid down her neck, to her shoulder, and down her chest until his fingers grazed the top of her breast. She moaned into his mouth. And then he had both hands on her breasts, rubbing her nipples through the silk, making her ache between her legs. She wrapped her arms around his neck as he continued to toy with her breasts, his mouth on hers. His head wrenched up at the sound of a knob twisting. They both turned to see a door open that she hadn't noticed before, as it blended in with the dark paneling on the far side of the room.

"Through here, James. And hurry," a tall man said.

James grabbed her hand and pulled her quickly to the open door. As it closed, they both heard the main entrance to the room open. "Lucinda?" she heard her father say.

"Best straighten your dress, miss," the tall man said.

"Eyes up, MacAvoy," James said.

She glanced down at herself and turned quickly away. She pulled her dress into place and turned back. "So this is MacAvoy."

"This is MacAvoy."

"Thank you," she said.

"How did you know where to find us?"

"Was keeping an eye on you and her da. The way he was looking at you, boyo, you're lucky you're not dead. Eleanor saw the two of you come out of the servants' door to the gallery, and I had a good idea what your intentions were."

"There's a lady present, MacAvoy. Best not take that thought any further."

She laughed and looked up at James's friend. "Thank you, Mr. MacAvoy. Do you have a plan for how to get us back into the party?"

"Not Mr. MacAvoy. Just MacAvoy. Eleanor, my betrothed," he said and straightened, preening as he said the woman's name, "will take you up the servants' staircase so you can come down the public one."

Just then the door opened to the hallway, and James pushed her behind him. A tall, attractive woman in the conservative uniform of a servant stepped inside.

"Mrs. Emory," James said.

"Mr. Thompson. It appears you need rescuing yet again," she said and turned to Lucinda. "Miss, we're going directly across the hall to a servants' door. Follow me, please."

Lucinda touched her hand to his as she hurried behind the woman now leading her confidently out the door. Lucinda stopped at the entrance before entering the hallway to look for her father.

"Mr. Vermeal is with Mr. and Mrs. Nathan Pendergast, miss," Mrs. Emory said over her shoulder. "This way, please."

Lucinda followed her to another cleverly hidden door that Mrs. Emory swung open, disappearing to Lucinda's left up a set of steep steps. She could hear the chatter of servants and the clang of pots and pans from the descending staircase. They exited a similarly hidden door as she followed the woman to a wide and quiet hallway.

"Perhaps you'd like to check your dress in here, miss, before I take you to the ladies' retiring room down the hall," the woman said and opened a door to a bedroom.

Lucinda hurried inside and turned to a wood-framed full-length mirror. Her hair needed repairing, and she did as best as she could without Giselle, repinning several curls that had come loose. She yanked her chemise back into place, adjusted her corset as best as she could, and then straightened the silk folds of her dress at her bosom. It would have to do, she thought, and hurried to the door.

"Follow me, miss," Mrs. Emory said.

"Thank you very much." Lucinda slipped into the room the woman indicated.

Muriell Thompson stood at one of the mirrors set up in the room and looked up when Lucinda walked in. Lucinda glanced in the mirror beside her and touched her hair with her fingertips.

"Miss Thompson."

"Miss Vermeal."

They turned to the door at the same time. Lucinda had no choice but to walk side by side with James's sister.

"Mrs. Pendergast has hosted a lovely party," Lucinda said as they descended the stairs.

"She has."

Lucinda drew a breath and glanced ahead of her at the bottom of the steps. Her father stood there, tapping a finger on the newel post. She stopped when she reached the bottom step, smiling up at him, fully expecting Miss Thompson to continue on her way. But she did not.

"Hello, Papa. Are you enjoying yourself?"

"Where have you been? I've been looking everywhere for you for at least thirty minutes."

"I was upstairs in the ladies' retiring room, if you must know," she said and pursed her lips. "How gauche I am to mention it."

Miss Thompson slipped her hand through Lucinda's arm. "Miss Vermeal and I were enjoying a chat. I'm terribly sorry to have worried you, sir."

Lucinda could barely believe her eyes, and if her father's face was any indication, he did not believe her at all.

"Have you been introduced, Papa? This is Mrs. Elspeth Pendergast's sister, Miss Muireall Thompson."

"I have not," he said and nodded to her.

"It was lovely chatting," Miss Thompson said to her and walked away from them, back to the room where everyone was still having dessert and coffee.

CHAPTER 8

"Saw Jackson fight yesterday."

"What? He's in Philadelphia now?" James asked.

"Took the train to New York. Going to take my fare out of our next winnings," MacAvoy said.

James stopped punching the sand-filled leather bag swinging in front of him. "You what?"

"Went to New York. Heard some rumors this kid was the real deal and wanted to see for myself."

"Well? What did you find out?" James asked as he wiped his face with a length of toweling.

"He's good."

James turned. MacAvoy was looking at him steadily. He was not one to exaggerate or make false claims. He just told the truth as he saw it. "How good?"

MacAvoy took a breath. "Good enough."

"I'll just have to make sure I'm better."

MacAvoy stared at him, not speaking until James began to hit the swinging leather again. He let the rhythm of his punches and the ensuing sound as he battered his fists against the heavy bag take him to the place where his concentration, his intent, canceled out all distractions. Sweat flew from his hair and ran down his back as he forced his tired legs to keep moving and bouncing. He lost track of time, where he was, how long he'd been thrusting his arms, until his knees shook with the effort to remain upright. He stopped, swaying on his feet, eyes closed while he fought to catch his breath. He would be ready for Jackson, one way or another. Two weeks. He had two weeks.

* * *

"Where am I taking you?" James asked Kirsty. Her eyes were lit with anticipation, and maybe nervousness, which was unlike her.

"To the University of Pennsylvania. I'm to meet Elspeth and Alexander there." She held a hand against her stomach, taking short breaths. "Muireall will be furious if I go alone. You must take me."

"Of course, Kirsty. Don't get yourself upset. I'll take you." He laid a hand on her shoulder. "What has you in such a fit?"

"Nothing. Nothing. I'm fine, James. How do I look?"

"Kirsty! Sweetheart. Tell me what has you all aflutter?"

"Oh, James! Alexander's college friend. I met him at Elspeth's party. He took me into dinner. He's speaking tonight at the College of Medicine. Speaking! Alexander thought we might go to support him."

"Well, then, we should go," he said and smiled at her. "What is his name?"

"Albert. His name is Albert."

"Does he have a last name?"

"Oh yes. His name is Albert Watson. He's British!"

"Kirsty, you must relax. We're going to have to take the street-car. I would have rented a carriage for tonight if I'd known," James said. "Why didn't Alexander come for you?"

"I told them I wasn't going," she said.

"But we're going now?"

"Yes, James!" she said, her eyes wide. "I'm not a coward. Please hurry and get your coat."

Amazingly, they found Elspeth and Alexander outside the doors to the lecture hall. Kirsty clung to her sister while he and Alexander shared a smile. Just as they were going into the building, he heard his sister's name, and they turned in unison.

"Mrs. Pendergast?"

"Hello! How lovely to see you again," Elspeth said to Louisa Vermeal, nodding to the man beside her.

"Mr. Pendergast. Mr. Thompson. Miss Thompson. May I present a dear friend of mine, Mr. Renaldo Delgado, recently of Spain. These young people are two of his children, Geoffrey and Susannah."

"Are you going into the lecture?" Alexander asked.

Mr. Delgado nodded. "Geoffrey is very interested in the subject and is considering a career in medicine or science."

"How long will you be in Philadelphia?" Elspeth asked.

"Perhaps another month," Mr. Delgado said and glanced at Lucinda's aunt.

"Are you enjoying your visit?" Elspeth asked his children.

"Yes, ma'am. Thank you for asking," the young man said to Elspeth, who turned to the daughter.

"I heard your party was a grand success and that your artwork collection is very lovely," she said quietly.

"Thank you! Why don't you come visit my husband and I some evening?" Elspeth said as she looked at the group. "Or perhaps you and Miss Vermeal can come for tea in the afternoon and leave the menfolk behind."

The girl's eyes lit up, and she looked at Lucinda's aunt.

"I think we would enjoy that very much, wouldn't we, Susannah?" Miss Vermeal replied.

"We'd best go in," Kirsty said. "We don't want to be late. It was very nice meeting you."

* * *

"MACAVOY?" JAMES HOLLERED UP A SET OF STEPS IN THE carriage house behind Elspeth and Alexander's house. "MacAvoy? Are you here?"

"James? Come up. Come up and see."

James walked up the flight of steps beyond a ground-floor door surrounded by an arch of roses. He could smell soap as he ascended and heard the chatter of a young child. He stepped into a large room where MacAvoy was painting walls. Various buckets of paint and mops and rags were scattered around the room. A little girl, her long hair plaited, in a paint-stained dress and pinafore, glanced up at him and ran at MacAvoy. He scooped her up in one arm and kissed her forehead.

"Mary, sweetheart, no need to be scared. This is my very best friend. His name is Mr. Thompson."

The child clung to his neck and peeped out at James.

"It's an honor to meet you, Mary." James smiled at the little girl, a miniature of her mother. She shimmied down MacAvoy's side, picked up a rag doll, and kissed its face. "What are you doing painting in Elspeth's carriage house?"

"I've been meaning to tell you," MacAvoy went on excitedly. "Eleanor and Mary and I are going to live here once we're married. Alexander has been intending for a few years to fix it up for an employee, but he'd never gotten around to it. Elspeth suggested he rent it to us so Eleanor is close to her work. I can easily afford the rent and still save for a house. And there's a small Catholic church two blocks away with a school. Mary can go there next year and learn her letters."

MacAvoy led him through the large room, telling him where Eleanor intended to put their table and chairs and how sofas and overstuffed chairs would sit near the fireplace for them to sit together as a family after a long day of work. He showed him the bedrooms, one large and two smaller ones, and the other room where a stove and icebox would go when they arrived. A workman was building cupboards and running pipes for the water in the kitchen and in the bathing room. It would be cozy and perfect for MacAvoy's small family.

James stood in the center of the room and made a slow turn. "It's going to be perfect, MacAvoy."

The next thing he knew he was wrapped up in MacAvoy's long arms, hugging him, his friend's fists pounding his back. MacAvoy released him and wiped at his face, his lip trembling.

"I never thought I'd have anything to call my own. Not a fancy flat like this or a woman willing to be my missus or a precious little girl. I never thought or expected it. If it weren't for you and your family, I never would have," MacAvoy said.

"You would have done fine without us."

MacAvoy shook his head. "I don't think so. Ma never really took any notice of me other than to filch her a bottle of gin. It was the Locust Street house where I learned what a family looked like, what respect was, what hard work got you, and when Ma died, I'd have been living on the street and she would have been resting in a pauper's grave if it hadn't been for all of you."

"You've got to give yourself some credit too, MacAvoy. You worked hard and did your schooling even when things were bad at your house. I remember you hungry and cold in too-small clothes, but you kept your chin up, and that's why you have Mrs. Emory willing to marry you, a good job at the mill, and you're the best corner man in any boxing ring on the East Coast. You did it, MacAvoy. You had some help, but you did it."

"Malcolm? Have you given our guest a tour?" Mrs. Emory said from the doorway. Mary ran to her and nearly disappeared in her voluminous skirts. "How are you today, Mr. Thompson?"

"Well, Mrs. Emory. Thank you," he said. "This is going to be a perfect spot for you and MacAvoy. Congratulations. My sister thinks the world of you."

"Mrs. Pendergast is a delight to know and to work for. Is there anything I can help you with? I've just stopped by to check on my painting crew." She smiled at a grinning MacAvoy.

"I've just come to drop off tickets for my next match for Alexander. Is he home?"

"Yes. He's in his study. Would you like me to come in with you?" she asked.

"I know the way," he said and nodded to his friend and Mrs. Emory.

James made his way to the back of his sister's massive home. He wondered if he'd see her beating rugs with the maids or peeling potatoes with the kitchen staff as he stepped through the servants' door and up the steps to the family's floors. He went down the long, wide carpeted hallway toward his brother-in-law's office and heard his sister's voice coming from a room on his right. He hurried to the open door and looked inside. Elspeth stood near the entrance with her back to him, examining a piece of paper. He picked her up, twirled her around, and dropped a loud smacking kiss on her cheek.

"James! You devil, you! You scared me!" she said after shrieking with laughter.

"How is my favorite sister? Now don't you go telling Muireall or Kirsty I said that!" James said.

"I'm fine. Wonderful," she said. "And enjoying some lovely female company."

James tilted his head at his sister and turned as she began to walk farther into the room toward the fireplace and seating area. It was then he realized they were not alone. His eyes lit immediately on Lucinda Vermeal.

"You are blushing, Mr. Thompson," she said.

Elspeth laughed. "Do you remember Miss Susannah Delgado from our meeting at the college, James? And of course, Miss Vermeal and Miss Vermeal."

"I do," he said and pulled his flat cap from his head. "It's a pleasure to see you all again, ladies."

"Won't you join us, Mr. Thompson?" Louisa Vermeal said. "We've exhausted all the female conversation."

"Did I hear a shout from this direction?" Alexander asked from the doorway.

"Perhaps a shout of desperation since we've asked Mrs. Pendergast's brother to join us for some conversation and tea," Louisa Vermeal said with a smile.

"It was me shouting, Alexander," Elspeth said. "James snuck up on me and frightened the wits out of me!"

"Won't you join us too, Mr. Pendergast?" Louisa asked.

LUCINDA WAS ENJOYING HIS DISCOMFORT, AND SHE THOUGHT HE knew it too. He was embarrassed to be caught surprising his sister and certainly hoping to elicit a shout from her, which he had. She'd swallowed a lump in her throat when he twirled his sister around and kissed her cheek. How marvelous to be so . . . open, so obvious with one's feelings. She'd been taught all of her life to be demure and restrained. James Thompson was the very opposite. She loved that about him and envied him as well, even though Aunt Louisa was everything any daughter could want. There would never be any doubt in James's sisters' or his brother's minds that he loved them unequivocally.

He made his way to the small sofa and sat down beside her, making her move her skirts so that they were not trapped under his leg. His sister reseated herself beside Susannah Delgado and her aunt while Mr. Pendergast leaned against the mantelpiece.

"Just had a tour of your carriage house. It's going to work out well for MacAvoy and Mrs. Emory," he said.

"I'm so pleased we could make this arrangement for them," Elspeth said and glanced at her husband, who smiled at her fondly.

Lucinda glanced at James and raised her brows.

"Elspeth and Alexander are fixing the second floor of the

carriage house for them to live in once they are married. MacAvoy showed me every nook of the place and their plans for it." He looked at her steadily. "Would you like to see it?"

"I believe I would."

He stood and offered her his hand to stand and then tucked hers around his forearm. "If you'll excuse us for a few minutes."

They walked down a long hallway, down a set of steps, and to the carriage house at the back of the property. It was a large building, with open doors at the bottom, all shaded by a massive tree. She followed him up the steps and through an open door.

"MacAvoy? Mrs. Emory?" he said and turned to her. "They must have finished their painting and cleaning for the day."

"It's a lovely room with these large windows," she said and looked around.

"It is," he whispered and stepped close to her. "We'll have to get a tour another day. MacAvoy is proud as punch and wants to show it off."

"By all means," she said and glanced at his mouth.

He picked up her hand and kissed her knuckles, then twisted her arm behind her, pulling her flush against him, from her breasts to her thighs. She laid her other hand on his chest, feeling the strong, rapid beat of his heart under her palm. She licked her lips as he watched and heard him expel a short breath.

"I'm going to kiss you, Lucinda, and I'd like to do more."

He moved his head closer to her, not quite touching her lips with his, but she could feel his breath on her cheek. She closed her eyes, drinking in the fragrance of him, something spicy and earthy, and felt him hard against her stomach through his pants and her dress and petticoats. She rubbed her hips up once against him and realized she was panting as if she'd climbed three flights of stairs—or was terrified.

"What would you like to do, James?" she whispered against his mouth.

He moved his mouth to her ear and ran his tongue around its

shell. "Well, I suppose I should say I want to make love to you, to touch your naked body with mine, let down all that beautiful hair, press those pale breasts against my chest, and whisper love words to you. And I do want to do that and more, but it would be easier and more accurate for me to say I want to fuck you till you shout my name."

She'd only heard that word once before, years ago, a lament from a driver, when she had been traveling and their coach lost a wheel.

She knew what it meant. She knew it was crude. But when James Thompson whispered in her ear, his words, oh, that word made her breasts tight and made her squirm against him. She moaned; she couldn't help herself. He covered her mouth with his and held her tight to him. She pressed her hands to his face, his beard rough under her fingers, and slipped her hands into his hair, that dark, silky hair that drew her. She opened her eyes a fraction.

He was staring at her as he ran his tongue around the inside curve of her lips. Why this man? Why did this man's touch make her yearn and let down her feminine guard to the degree that she didn't care what others thought of her? Didn't care that Edith had spread some innuendoes about her to their friends? Didn't care if other men viewed her as less than virginal if they witnessed the lasciviousness of this embrace?

"James?" they both heard from the stairs below.

He held her close to him, one arm firmly around her waist. "I'm here, Elspeth."

"Miss Vermeal and Miss Delgado are getting ready to go. Perhaps you and Miss Vermeal should come inside."

He chuckled against her hair and whispered, "My sister knows exactly what is going on and is far too genteel to mention it." He turned his head. "Coming, Elspeth."

"What is going on here?" she asked and looked up at him from under her lashes.

His eyes slid from hers. "Just some harmless kisses. They don't mean anything."

She pulled herself away from him. "Of course they don't," she said and looked at him steadily.

* * *

JAMES PICKED UP THE WEIGHTS AND BROUGHT THEM SLOWLY TO his chest, concentrating on pushing his muscles and not on Lucinda Vermeal when she agreed his kisses meant nothing. Granted, he'd been less than honest with her at the time. He knew they were not harmless kisses. He remembered how those lips teased him, showing him what he'd never have, what he'd never be worthy of, how furious he'd been when she denied their power.

"What do you think, MacAvoy?" he asked, hoping to rid himself of his anger.

"Better."

"Better? I'm in the best shape of my life," James said after dropping the weights to the floor.

"You're looking good," MacAvoy said.

James wiped a towel down his face and around his neck. "But not good enough, huh, MacAvoy?"

"Don't be an ass. You know there's nothing good about being overconfident. I'm telling you, you look good. But so does Jackson."

"Overconfident? Who said anything about being overconfident? I always take my bouts seriously. I take my opponents seriously!"

"Calm down, James," MacAvoy said and looked around at the other men training, all staring at them. "What are you looking at?" he shouted at one of them.

"I'm not a child. You don't have to treat me like one."

"The only time I treat you like a child is when you act like one."

"Fuck you," he said. "I don't need to be patronized by the likes of you."

MacAvoy's head snapped back as if James had hit him. He'd gone too far, he knew he had, but he couldn't stop himself.

"The likes of me," MacAvoy whispered.

"You're just one more that thinks I'm washed up! Thinks I'm not *the* James Thompson! Thinks I'm done for."

"That's not what I think, but maybe there's someone else you'd like in your corner."

James stared at his hands for a moment, trying to calm himself, but he couldn't. His anger was red-hot, and whether MacAvoy deserved his sharp tongue or not, it hardly mattered. He was alone, and he'd always be alone, whether he was winning matches or whether he was digging ditches, and he'd best get on with the reality of it all. And if he wasn't boxing, what would it matter? It was who he was. He looked up at MacAvoy.

"That's probably for the best," he said and walked away.

* * *

JAMES WAS SPRAWLED ACROSS HIS BED, SOAKING UP THE WINTER sun coming through his window and heating the sore muscles in his arms and shoulders. Even with the ointment Aunt Murdoch had made for him, he ached in the mornings until he could stretch out. He heard Mrs. McClintok telling Payden and Robert that breakfast was on the table. His stomach grumbled, and he swung his legs over the edge of the bed, taking his time pulling his arms over his head, letting the stiffness ease out. There was less than a week until his Jackson match, and he would only do one more intense workout before then, finishing the week with light exercise and massages.

He was afraid there was no recovering from the argument he'd had with MacAvoy. And knowing that it was his own bad temper that caused it made it twice as bad in his own head. He was embarrassed by his behavior but hard-pressed to admit it. He'd told no one that Billy Pettigrew would now be in his corner.

James seated himself at the large wooden kitchen table where he and the other early risers in his family often had breakfast, although the boys must have already eaten. Mrs. McClintok brought him a plate piled high with eggs, ham, and bread toasted in the oven. She moved a jar of plum jelly close to his plate.

"Coffee, Mr. Thompson?"

"Shouldn't you be calling me James since we're cousins?"

"No, I shouldn't. Cousins or not, I'm the Thompson housekeeper. It wouldn't be proper."

He nodded and smiled. "Coffee, thank you, Mrs. McClintok."

The kitchen door opened, and Elspeth came in, greeting Mrs. McClintok as she did and waving James back into his seat. She bent over and kissed his cheek.

"Tea, Mrs. Pendergast?"

"Yes, thank you, Mrs. McClintok."

"Aren't you looking lovely this morning?" he said as she seated herself beside him.

"Thank you, James," she said. "I'm feeling well finally after a few weeks of . . . of being under the weather."

"Are you sick, Elspeth?" He laid down his fork. "What is the matter? Do you need to see the doctor? Why hasn't Alexander taken you to the doctor?"

She smiled at him and laid her fingers on his arm. "I'm fine, James."

"Morning sickness, Mrs. Pendergast?" Mrs. McClintok asked.

Elspeth nodded and blushed. "It seems to have gone away, just as the doctor said it would."

"Oh," James said. "This is normal for ladies who are expecting?"

"Not all ladies, Mr. Thompson, but many."

"That is not why I came over this morning," Elspeth said and looked at James. "Truly, I feel fine now, and the doctor said it is very common."

"What do you need, then?" James asked, relieved that his sister was fine and that he did not need to know any more about the subject.

Elspeth stirred sugar into her tea and took a sip. She looked up at him. "Mrs. Emory told me you fired MacAvoy. Is that true, James?"

He stared at his plate, moving the last of the eggs onto his fork with the crust of his bread. It hadn't occurred to him until recently that his family may have something to say about that subject, as they were nosy and opinionated.

He shrugged. "It's not anything for you to be concerned about."

"Not anything for me to be concerned about? How ridiculous! MacAvoy is as much a part of the Thompson family as any of us. What are the two of you arguing about?"

"Boxing, is all. Nothing really."

"I don't believe that for one second, and neither does Alexander. What has happened?"

James pushed back from the table, his eyes on the coffee cup he held in his hand. How could he tell her, or any of them, but especially her, who'd always had a special place in his heart? How could he tell her he was terrified of what the future might bring? That he'd imagined he'd always be twenty-five years old and handsome and fit and unbeatable in a ring? Could he tell anyone that he recognized a massive change in his life on the horizon and could not accept it? Would not accept it. Would rather ignore it, regardless of what a fool it made him.

"There's nothing to say." He shrugged. "We had a parting of the ways. It happens, Elspeth. People drift apart."

He glanced at her face, at the pity he saw there, and the love too, and lurched to his feet. "I've got to be going. Got to get ready for my next match. How are you getting home, Elspeth?"

She stood and touched his face. "I love you so dearly, James. You're always concerned about me and all of our family. My carriage is outside. I'll be fine."

He watched her leave the kitchen, his throat aching, his heart pounding. Mrs. McClintok was staring at him steadily when he turned his head. "More eggs or toast, Mr. Thompson?"

He shook his head, hurried up the steps and through his bedroom door. They all had to stick their female noses in his business, and he did not care for it. He pulled on his jacket, ran down the steps and out the front door, heading to the workout rooms without saying a word to anyone in his family. He would punch heavy bags and maybe some poor idiot's face until he felt more himself.

CHAPTER 9

"Perhaps we shouldn't say anything to her about it," Lucinda heard her aunt say as she stopped by the parlor doorway to fix her hem that had caught on the buckle of her shoe. She and Aunt were at the Pendergast house again with Susannah Delgado, enjoying an afternoon visit. She hadn't visited Edith for weeks and was the better for it, she was convinced. She straightened and flounced her skirts, making sure they would not catch again.

"Although James would not care for it, I think Miss Vermeal should know. I think she may be able to talk some sense into him," Elspeth Pendergast said.

Lucinda walked in and noticed Susannah at the far end of the room, stretched out on the floor with several books. Lucinda glanced at her aunt and Elspeth before sitting down.

"If there is any doubt in either of your minds, I did hear part of your conversation," she said and reached for her tea on the small table beside her. "What should I know?"

"Perhaps you should tell her, Mrs. Pendergast," Aunt said.

"Have you been introduced to Malcolm MacAvoy, Miss Vermeal?" Elspeth asked after a long moment.

"I have," Lucinda said and thought back to the party right

here in this house where she'd been stolen away during dessert and James had kissed and caressed her. "I understand that he works for your brother."

"Not exactly. You see, MacAvoy—his name is Malcolm, but we all call him MacAvoy—

lived with us on Locust Street after his mother died, God rest her soul, and even before that he and James were together constantly. He works at my husband's family's textile factory on the river and is James's cornerman, his ring man, at the boxing matches."

"What is a cornerman?" Aunt Louisa asked.

"MacAvoy sets up the matches and watches the opponent before their match with James to study their style and see if he can identify weaknesses. At the bell during the matches, he patches up cuts on James's face or stuffs his nose with cotton if his nose is bloodied. He keeps him focused during a match on what his strategy is," Elspeth said.

"He gets cut during these matches?" Lucinda asked. "On his face? That's where the scars on his face are from, aren't they?"

Aunt's brows were raised, and Lucinda admitted to herself she was horrified when Elspeth nodded. She'd never seen a boxing match and didn't believe she ever wanted to.

"And people attend these matches, do they?" Aunt Louisa asked.

"Oh yes," Elspeth said. "They are very well attended—all men, of course. That is one reason James has made so much money at it, even after giving MacAvoy his cut. Men come from far away and fill the stands to see him fight. I don't know how it all works, but he gets some amount from the admission the men pay to attend, and then, of course, he gets the prize money if he wins, which he does. Win, that is."

"He always wins?" Lucinda asked.

Elspeth nodded. "From his very first match when he was eighteen years old."

"What is it that you have not told me?" she asked.

"He fired MacAvoy last week. I found out from Mrs. Emory, our housekeeper."

"James showed me the rooms they are redoing over your carriage house for after they are married the last time we visited."

Elspeth nodded. "Yes. That is right."

"What did Mrs. Emory tell you?"

"She said that MacAvoy is devastated, mostly over their friendship ending, but she says he is worried that James will be reckless in the ring without him there. She said that MacAvoy said this Jackson fellow that James is set to fight is the best boxer he's ever seen other than James. He said James has not been right for several weeks, and MacAvoy believes it is because of something my husband, Alexander, said to him."

"Something Mr. Pendergast said?" Aunt Louisa asked.

"I know what it is." Lucinda turned to her aunt. "The day that you helped Mrs. Pendergast's sister with a dress for their dinner party, he and I sat in the park on a bench while he ate a sandwich from a vendor. He told me that Mr. Pendergast had proposed some kind of gymnasium or arena for matches and for him to manage it. He said these men, these investors, think he's washed up. I told him they most likely see a winning horse and wish to bet on him."

"He was insulted by their proposal?" Aunt asked.

"I believe he was. Deeply insulted," Mrs. Pendergast said. "I told my husband I'd wished he'd talked to me before he talked to James about this."

"And why is that, Mrs. Pendergast?" she asked.

"I could have suggested he approach James in a different manner. He is the emotional heart of our family, you see. Muireall is very busy running the household, seeing to our youngest brother's education, and managing the finances that our family relies on. Kirsty and I did as we were told, but we both knew, and Payden too, that James would guard us, guide us, and always stand up for us. He's been the father figure for all of us, even though he's only a few years older than me."

"How long have your parents been gone, Mrs. Pendergast?" Aunt asked.

She stared out the window before turning back to them both. "My parents died on the passage here on the steamer we took from Port Charlotte in Scotland in 1855. They were most likely murdered."

Aunt Louisa gasped. "Oh dear! How dreadful!"

"I'm guessing you know something of my family's history," Mrs. Pendergast said to Lucinda.

She nodded. "Not much, and I'm not sure of its accuracy, considering the source. I've been told you were the victim of violence prior to your marriage."

"I'm certain that is not all that you heard." Mrs. Pendergast smiled. "You're being diplomatic, I think. I'm going to tell you both some of the history of the Thompson family that we do not share widely."

"You have no worries from either of us, Mrs. Pendergast," Aunt said. "Confidences are respected."

"I expected they were. You see, my father was the ninth Earl of Taviston. A Scottish title," she said. "Our family and properties were threatened by a man who felt the earldom should have been his. Father meant to get us to safety for a year or two until his case could be proven, as this man had produced false documents that, even though they were false, still had to be examined."

"Mr. Thompson is the earl?" Aunt Louisa asked.

"No. He's actually our cousin. His parents died when he was but an infant, and he was raised by my mother and father. Payden is the tenth earl."

"But you refer to him as your brother," Lucinda said.

Elspeth smiled. "He *is* my brother."

"And that has something to do with why you were a victim of violence?"

"I was kidnapped and held to be exchanged for Payden."

"Oh, dear Lord," Aunt Louisa said. "You must have been terrified!"

"I was, but I knew my duty, and I knew the Thompsons would never give up Payden, the true Earl of Taviston. I would either be rescued or die. I managed to kill a man," she said and took a deep breath, "and injure another before James and Alexander came for me. I was determined to give them any advantage I could, even . . . even if it meant . . . whatever it meant, I would do it."

Lucinda could not help but admire her. Even with her blushes and shyness and soft voice, she was very much a woman who had steel in her spine. "I am in awe of your courage, Mrs. Pendergast."

"Trust me, I was frightened out of my wits," she said and then shrugged. "But duty was ingrained in us from early childhood. And James views his duty as physical; he protects his family. The boxing is just an extension of how he sees himself. He is most intimidating in the ring and when challenged to defend us, and his bouts are part of a mystique, I think, that he is unbeatable. That he is the impenetrable wall that surrounds us."

"So when your husband suggested that he begin to prepare for when he would not be able to win every match with a new endeavor, he understood them to think that he was no longer that wall of protection surrounding his sisters and brother," Lucinda said.

"That is exactly how I think James has interpreted it. He's angry and hurt and, I think, afraid to think about the next chapter of his life. MacAvoy told him a few weeks ago that he was going to take on more side work when he's not at the mill in preparation for when James would not be boxing as much."

"He would feel betrayed," Lucinda said softly.

"Yes, I believe he would."

"When is his next match?"

"Friday. This Friday. Alexander and MacAvoy are going."

"Perhaps I can arrange to speak to him before then," Lucinda said and glanced at her aunt, now watching her closely.

"I don't know if it would be helpful or not, but I wish you would. You are not family, not involved in boxing, but he seems, well, connected to you somehow," Mrs. Pendergast said.

"We have had a few occasions for conversation. I find him refreshingly honest."

"And ridiculously handsome," Aunt said with a laugh.

"He is that!" Mrs. Pendergast said as Susannah joined them, apparently done with her reading.

* * *

"Have Giselle pack your trunk for a few days," her father said as they sat down to dinner that evening. "I'd like you to come as well, Louisa. She'll need a female chaperone. Unless, of course, you intend to ignore your duty to spend your time with that Delgado fellow and leave your niece at sixes and sevens."

"What are you talking about, Henri? There are no travel plans that I'm aware of," Louisa replied.

"I have just finalized the arrangements. We leave tomorrow morning."

"When are we returning, Papa?"

"We'll return Friday evening,"

Aunt glanced at her. "Could we not return Friday morning, Henri? I've plans for Friday evening."

"Not the morning. Perhaps the afternoon, if my business is concluded."

Lucinda cleared her throat. "Why would we be accompanying you on a business trip, Papa?"

He laid down his fork and knife and looked at her. "Because you are my daughter. Because I enjoy having you with me. Because there will be some interesting people to meet. We'll take the train at nine and be in Valley Forge by luncheon."

She buttered her croissant and looked at her aunt, who shook her head. She agreed. There would be no changing his mind, and an argument would only make the days miserable. She would not have an opportunity to speak to James before his match. But if they were back in time, she was going to see James fight. She would see him for herself and perhaps talk to him afterward.

* * *

"WON'T YOU WALK OUTSIDE WITH ME, MISS VERMEAL? THE night is fine," Carlton Young asked.

"No, thank you, Mr. Young," Lucinda said to the host's son. It was Thursday of the week spent with her father and aunt at the Young home—mansion, really—set on the banks of the Schuylkill River in Valley Forge. They were three of the more than thirty guests who'd been feted with endless rich foods and wine, entertainment, and the chance to mingle with their equals in wealth and social standing. She'd been to any number of these sorts of entertainments in Virginia, and this bore a close resemblance, even down to the similarity of the types of guests. The haughty, some hoping to further their social standing, the beautiful, the well-educated, and of course, those looking to cement future relationships, whether they were of a business nature or more personal. Mr. Young was looking at Lucinda as his prize.

"Let me get your wrap, my dear," he said with a smile.

She looked back at him steadily. "No, thank you."

"What a charming couple you make," Mrs. Young said as she approached and patted her son's arm. "Like a romantic portrait with you standing in front of the fireplace."

"Lucinda," Aunt said, surely offering to rescue her. "Would you like to take a turn about the room with me? There are several paintings we could enjoy discussing."

She smiled. "I'm fine, Aunt Louisa."

And she was fine. She was not some inexperienced and naive

debutante easily manipulated by the likes of Mrs. Young and her son. She looked directly at her hostess.

"Your comment was inappropriate, ma'am. Mr. Young and I are not a couple nor was there any intent on my part to be an element in a *romantic* scene, as you have implied."

She was gratified to see the spark of anger behind Mrs. Young's ever-present smile of condescension and glanced at her son. He was looking at Lucinda with fawning admiration. Mrs. Young drifted away to another guest, and Father joined them, looking from Carlton Young to her and back again with a smile.

Mr. Young made his feelings known at that moment. "Miss Vermeal. I am . . . I am in awe of you. No one ever stands up to my mother. Your set down was magnificent. Allow me to fetch you some lemonade or wine."

Lucinda did not roll her eyes. Aunt Louisa did. Carlton Young was a tall, handsome man, schooled at the best colleges with a year spent traveling in Europe to add a certain panache he hoped to exude. He was also easily managed and accustomed to a woman directing his every move. He was the quintessential husband for her, per her father's requirements.

"What have you done?" he asked as Mr. Young hurried away to retrieve refreshments.

"Done?" Lucinda asked. "No more than you would have expected me to. Mrs. Young's implications were ridiculous and involved our family name. Certainly, you would not wish me to embroil the Vermeals in something that could be tawdry."

Henri Vermeal's face was red, and his lips trembled with rage. "He is the perfect choice for you, Lucinda. I've already decided. He will give you attractive children, has just the right pedigree, and you will be able to handle him with little effort. Insulting his mother will not smooth the way!"

"Henri," Aunt Louisa said with a smile. "Keep your voice down. Others are watching. And while you would be insulted if someone belittled your mother, apparently Carlton Young is not.

In fact, it has made him fall even more in love with Lucinda, although she does not return his regard."

Henri took a deep breath and turned to Lucinda. "You will consider this man as your husband and remember that I only want the best for you and am more understanding of the realities of the world. You do not wish to disappoint me, do you, Daughter?"

The sad truth was she did not wish to disappoint him, but she would not be tied to Carlton Young, regardless of how much guilt and pressure her father applied. Mr. Young returned just then, juggling several glasses.

"I wasn't sure what you or your aunt would like," he said. "I have lemonade, wine, and punch."

Aunt took a glass of punch and handed Lucinda the lemonade.

"Thank you, Mr. Young," Lucinda said.

He was staring at her worshipfully. "Is there anything else I can get for your comfort?"

Her father laid a hand on his shoulder. "Why don't you and your parents plan on coming to visit us in Philadelphia? My daughter could show you around the city, with her aunt as a chaperone, of course."

"My schedule is quite—" Aunt Louisa began.

"I'm sure you'll find the time to help your beloved niece entertain a guest. What do you say, young man?"

He gulped. "I . . . I am honored, sir."

Lucinda let out a breath. There would be no escaping this association unless she took matters into her own hands. And what did that mean exactly?

* * *

"I haven't seen much of you, James," Muireall said from where she sat behind the desk in her small office. "Won't you come in? I was just finishing the bookkeeping."

The very last thing James wanted was to have a conversation with his older sister. He had hoped to walk by her open door without her notice. But even with her eyes firmly on the large open account book with the pale green pages and the tiny, tiny numbers she'd written, she knew he'd been hurrying past and aimed to stop him.

"I've got some things to prepare for tonight. Don't have much time."

"This will only take a few minutes." She looked up after she blew on a page to dry the ink. "Won't you sit down?"

He was hoping she'd not make him angry, even knowing it was in his control to get up and leave her office if she did. MacAvoy had told him countless times that anger was detrimental to his abilities in the ring, and he was right. He wanted—no, he needed a clear, calm head tonight as he'd be virtually on his own since Billy Pettigrew was as worthless as a cornerman as he was in the ring.

"I heard that you and MacAvoy had a falling out," Muireall said.

"We have."

"Probably for the best, James. He was never the caliber of individual the Thompsons should surround themselves with."

"That's rubbish, Muireall. He's been completely loyal to this family. He would lay his life down for any one of us."

Muireall shrugged. "Even so, his mother was nothing more than a drunk and perhaps loose with her favors when she was a young woman. He doesn't know who his father was."

"He worked hard, paid attention in school when he could go, and copied the manners and mannerisms of us so he would be able to better himself. Who are you to condemn a man for hard work and perseverance?"

"I don't know, James," she said and looked at him steadily. "Why did you have a falling out if you are so convinced of his value?"

James could feel himself get angry. He could feel his shoulders tense and his jaw clench. "You needn't goad me, Muireall. I know that's what you're doing, and I won't fall for it."

She rested her chin on her fisted hand, elbow on her desk. "What am *I* doing? I assume a cornerman is an important element in this boxing business that you insist on doing. What has happened for you to dismiss him from this and from your life?"

Muireall was the least emotional woman he'd ever encountered. Even when there'd been all the danger nearly two years ago with Elspeth and Payden, she'd maintained her dignity when she was, on that singular occasion, tearful. There was never a hint of false female emotion, like Kirsty was wont to do occasionally with some well-timed tears. At twelve years of age, Muireall had managed Aunt Murdoch and him and the girls, and wee Payden as well, as if she were a forty-year-old matron.

"I'll tell you about it after tonight. I promise. But thinking about it all upsets me, and I don't want to be upset going into this match. Jackson is good, maybe the best I've ever fought. I need to keep my head clear."

"Then by all means, go let this Jackson fellow plow his fist into your nose. I have complete faith in you to acquit yourself well. Aunt Murdoch and I will stay up in case you need a stitch or three. Best of luck, James."

She turned her attention back to her open account book, and James stood. It was time to get ready.

* * *

JAMES LAID DOWN ON THE FLOOR OF THE ROOM WHERE HE'D get changed for the fight. It was cold stone and smelled musty, but he'd had Billy sweep it clean and mop it the day before. Billy was standing outside the door now with strict orders to not allow anyone inside. James closed his eyes and let his mind quiet until all he could picture was a heavy leather bag swinging on chains from the rafters. He watched the bag, moved his mind's eye over each stitch and every imperfection in the leather, as it swung gradually left to right. His breathing slowed and his hands lay on the floor, his fingers neither stretched flat nor curled into a fist. Street sounds and noise from the arena, where workmen were setting up seating, faded away until all he heard was a distant hum.

In his head, he looked down at his hands, his fists clenched, his nails as short as he could trim them. He drew back his fist, feeling the power in his shoulder and arm and back, and moved toward its target. But then his arm dropped to his side, floating slowly down. He looked up, behind his closed eyes, looking for the heavy bag. But it was not there. There was a face instead. Lucinda Vermeal's face looking at him with sultry eyes and parted lips, as if he had just kissed her. Or more.

He sat straight up. Eyes open wide. The damn woman had invaded his quiet time. He stood, giving up on clearing his head, and opened the box that Aunt Murdoch had sent with him, full of thin strips of linen covered in a mixture of starch and cornmeal, something he'd never bothered with before. He dampened the strips and molded them to his upper teeth, one atop the other, until he had a thick pad. He held his jaw open as long as he could, letting them dry in their shape. James pulled the linen packing out and sat down to wait until it was time to dress for his match and stuff the foul-tasting fabric back in his mouth.

CHAPTER 10

Aunt Louisa stepped into her room and slowly closed the door. "What are you doing, Lucinda?" she whispered.

"I'm going to watch Mr. Thompson box. I'm going to talk to him if I can."

"You can hardly go alone, dear. There'll be hundreds of men, drinking liquor and in high spirits. It is far too dangerous for a young woman."

Lucinda laced up her flat-heeled boots. "I will keep to the edge of the room and mind my own business. Mrs. Pendergast said a few women attend. They like to place bets, from what I understand. I will be one of them."

"I shall send a note to Renaldo. He will escort you. I already told him that you may be asking this of him, and he said he would take you where you wanted to go."

"No. We will not involve Mr. Delgado. As kind as his offer is, I'll not ask him. It will only make matters worse between him and Papa. I've spoken to Laurent. His cousin has a carriage for hire. This cousin will take me and wait for me for however long I am there."

"Laurent is sure?"

"He is. He says Michael is a large fellow and would see that I am safe, would even go inside with me, if I should feel it necessary."

"You will knock on the wall between our dressing rooms the moment you are back."

"I will, Aunt," she said and kissed her on the cheek. "I promise."

Louisa grabbed her hands and held them tight. "I am so dreadfully worried about you, Lucinda. I am so concerned that I seriously considered going to your father and telling him what I suspected of your plans."

"You must do as you think best. But I am going to him. I fear that I'll soon be forced to choose between him and Papa. I don't know what has led me to this conclusion or why I'm willing to sacrifice my papa's good opinion, and maybe his love, but I am."

"You love him? This Mr. Thompson?"

"I'm not sure. I don't know what to think. But I do know that he intrudes on my thoughts at the strangest moments during the day and the night. I'm not sure I wish to kiss any man other than him. Ever."

"Then you must go. You must understand your feelings and if they are fleeting or if you think you will always feel the same. I wish I had been more courageous," she said. "And you must, you absolutely must, be very careful. I love you, dear."

"I love you too, Aunt. I will be very careful."

ALEXANDER AND MACAVOY WAITED WITH ALEXANDER'S father, Andrew, and his Uncle Nathan to enter the warehouse where James's match would be held. The line was long and rowdy, some men holding bottles of whiskey in their hands, and some occasionally shouting, although it was impossible to know what they were saying.

A young man staggered toward Nathan and held his half-full bottle at arm's length. "Want a drink, then, mate?" he said and hiccoughed.

"No. No, but thank you," Nathan said.

Alexander laughed as the two older men were enveloped into a group of young men.

"Will they get their pockets picked?" Alexander asked.

"Doubt it. I know some of those boys. They just like to carouse," MacAvoy said. "And we were never going to find four seats together anyway."

"Dear Lord!" Alexander said. "Father just took a swig out of that bottle."

"We're next," MacAvoy said as he nodded to the door of the warehouse. He pulled bills out of his trouser pockets, fumbling with the papers and dropping coins.

Alexander picked up the money. "Have you already been into those fellows' gin?" he said with a laugh and looked up. "What's the matter? You're not looking well."

MacAvoy blew out a breath. "I'm worried. It makes me sick thinking about James taking on Jackson without me in his corner. I'm not being proud or bragging, but I'm skilled at what I do for a boxer. Jackson is as good as James—and younger too. It's going to be brutal, and if I know James, he'll stay on his feet out of sheer stubbornness."

"Elspeth will never forgive me if something happens to him," Alexander said. "Is there anything you can do?"

"Not really, but I'd like to be in floor seats close to the ring. I'll be able to see what's going on."

Alexander and MacAvoy shouldered their way inside and headed to the betting tables, both laying down cash and taking their chits. MacAvoy found two young men in the second row near James's corner. He bodily picked them up and deposited them in a back row while Alexander eyed off anyone looking to try to take their seats.

"Have you seen your father and uncle?" MacAvoy asked.

"Over there. Uncle Nathan's the one struggling to climb up to the tiered seating. Good Lord. Father's pulling him up by his coat."

"That's what cheap gin does to you."

The crowd quieted when Red Chambliss, the promoter, in his purple jacket and green plaid pants, stepped into the ring.

"This match will go until one of the men is knocked out or doesn't make it back to the scratch, marked right here in the very center of the ring. No head butting, no spiked shoes, and no hitting a downed man at a Chambliss match. A round ends when a man's knee touches the floor, or he gets caught up in the ropes. Them corner men can carry him to his corner, and he's got thirty seconds, then I ring the bell, and he's got to get hisself to the scratch in eight seconds. We follow the London Prize Ring Rules," Chambliss said to hooting and hollering. "Except the ones we don't want to follow!"

The crowd roared when Jackson entered the warehouse. MacAvoy and Alexander stood with the rest of the men to see him as he made his way to the ring.

"Impressive specimen," Alexander shouted over the roar of the crowd.

"I saw him fight in New York a few months ago. Other than James, he's the best fighter I've ever seen."

The throng turned in their seats, and the noise increased three-fold. James Thompson had entered, and MacAvoy and Alexander were yelling and whistling along with the rest of the crowd. James was completely focused on his opponent, his eyes never leaving Jackson as he walked down an aisle created by shouting men, waving their hats and pumping their fists. His skin glistened in the glow of the gas lamps, his hair pushed back from his head, and the sash around his waist swaying as he walked. He went to the ring's stake closest to his corner and tied the strip of red-and-black plaid silk to the post.

"Both men have tied their colors! To your corners!" Chambliss shouted.

Thompson walked briskly to the man holding a jar of water beside Billy Pettigrew and took a drink. He turned with a flourish, making the crowd shout their approval, and stalked to the scratch, meeting Jackson in the middle of the ring. Chambliss rang a bell, and James threw a powerful punch into the chin of his opponent. But Jackson did not hesitate in his reply, knocking James back with punches to his midsection.

"You will wait here for me, Michael?" Lucinda asked the tall, heavy-set man helping her from the carriage near the warehouse where James was to fight. She'd been concerned she'd have to supply an address, but Laurent had assured her that Michael would know where the fight would be held. Every man in the city knew where the fight would be held, according to her butler.

"I'll be right here, miss. Unless you'll allow me to escort you inside. These matches attract a rowdy crowd."

"No. But thank you, Michael. If I'm uncomfortable, I'll come back out and get you."

"Just come out the door and wave my way. I'll keep an eye out for you. The whole thing shouldn't have you inside more than an hour."

"They fight for an hour?" she asked.

"No. But the fellow that runs these matches, Chambliss, he likes to build up the crowd to get them betting and liking the entertainment enough to come back. Usually, the fight itself only lasts but a quarter of an hour, but with Thompson fighting, sometimes it's over in minutes!"

"He is that good?"

"His fists fly so fast you can barely see them. It's a sight, miss, a real sight."

Lucinda held her bag against her waist and walked to the

entrance of the warehouse. She'd dressed in dark blue, a plain dress with the same color satin belt, a dark blue cloak—the only one she had without a fur collar—and a small hat covering her coiled blond hair with dark netting attached in the front, which she pulled down as she approached a huge man at the door.

"Fight's gonna be done soon, miss. You sure you want in? There be no returning any gate money."

Lucinda paid what he asked for and entered the room. It was like nothing she'd ever seen before, and she was glad she was dressed as she was, hoping to blend into the throng of men ahead of her. The room was warm and smelled of liquor and sweat; the noise was overwhelming and the crowd chaotic. She inched her way through men who were not paying any attention to her in the least. In fact, even when shouting and guzzling from a bottle, they pulled on the brims of their hats and caps as she maneuvered toward the ring. She could hear the sounds of flesh cracking against flesh and smell the sawdust, but she still could not see the fighting.

Lucinda tapped on a man's shoulder, hemmed in as she was on all sides by the surging crowd, and waited until he glanced at her. As he turned, she slipped in front of him and found herself at the end of long rows of benches. She looked up just in time to see James take a cruel blow from his opponent, sending blood and sweat from his mouth raining on the men in the front row. James returned the punches to the other man, drawing blood over his eye. The violence took her breath away. But there was something else that she could not draw her eyes from. It was James Thompson's bare chest, flexing as his fist flew at his opponent, his arms thick with roped, bulging muscle. His hands had blood on them, and she did not know if it was from the other man's nose or cuts on his knuckles. She glanced across the ring and saw MacAvoy pointing at her and nudging Alexander Pendergast beside him.

· · ·

"IS THAT MISS VERMEAL?" MACAVOY SAID AND POINTED.

"Good God! It is her! What is she doing here? We've got to get to her and escort her out of here. This is not a place for a woman."

"Like your wife?"

"At least Elspeth had the good sense to wear pants and hide her hair." Alexander stood. "I'll go for her."

MacAvoy pulled him back down to his seat. "Look at her, damn it!"

Lucinda Vermeal had stepped in front of the first row of the seated men, pardoning herself in the narrow space between them and the edge of the ring as the men pulled in their feet or stood, her arm and skirts brushing the ropes on the other side.

"If James catches sight of her, the match is over," MacAvoy said. "What's your clock saying?"

"Eighteen minutes. They've been fighting eighteen minutes," Alexander said and tucked his watch back in his pocket. "Without a bell."

"James is getting winded," MacAvoy said and screamed at Billy Pettigrew. "Tell him to take a knee!"

Miss Vermeal slipped behind the cornerman and made her way to them. Alexander took her outstretched hand and seated her beside MacAvoy. He knelt in the aisle close to her.

"What are you doing here, Miss Vermeal?" MacAvoy asked. "You'd best not let James see you here."

"It could be dangerous, Miss Vermeal," Alexander said. "Why don't you let me see you home?"

"There's no chance that Mr. Thompson could see me, MacAvoy. Both of his eyes are nearly swollen shut," she said. She was perched on the edge of the bench, her back straight, holding a little silk bag on her lap in gloved hands.

"He can see, miss."

"I was told these matches rarely last more than fifteen minutes. How long has this one been going on?" she asked.

Alexander pulled out his watch. "Twenty-two minutes."

THE CROWD QUIETED AS THE MATCH DRUG ON, MAKING THE sounds of fists hitting soft flesh magnified and making Lucinda feel nauseous. Both men were slowing down, in her opinion, and MacAvoy and Mr. Pendergast leaned in to talk to each other in front of her. She was pressed up to MacAvoy's side, and Mr. Pendergast's arm was against her hip.

"Trade places with me," MacAvoy finally said to Mr. Pendergast just as James took a swing at Jackson and missed completely, his opponent leaning out of the way and grabbing the rope. Jackson's knee barely grazed the floor, but a large man in a dreadfully colored suit who seemed to be in charge rang a bell. He must be the Chambliss fellow that Michael had mentioned. A young man ran into the ring at the sound of the bell and walked James back to the corner.

"Thirty seconds!" Chambliss shouted.

MacAvoy grabbed the man's shoulder. "Change in corner men, Chambliss."

An older man helping James's opponent shouted his displeasure.

"Shit on you, Bergman! I run the match. You can change corner men in my fights."

Men were exchanging money all around her, and she looked at Mr. Pendergast, who had moved her in on the bench and sat down on the end. He pulled her tight against him.

"What is going on? Is the fight over?"

"No. The fight isn't over. MacAvoy is going to run James's corner and maybe try and talk some sense into him."

James's chest was heaving with each breath, and his arms hung at his sides. MacAvoy pulled something from his mouth and another man held a jar of water to it. MacAvoy shoved the bloody thing back in his mouth and held James's head still, speaking to him, their foreheads touching. James straightened, rolled his neck, and turned back to the ring when the bell rang.

Both men seemed to benefit from the few moments away from the ring, but both began to slow down quickly. MacAvoy was shouting for James to take a knee as Mr. Pendergast looked at his watch.

"Twenty-six minutes," he said.

James landed a punch to the other man's stomach that doubled him over. Jackson, she'd heard the name over and again and knew it must be James's opponent, came up swinging while James's arms hung by his sides, surely trying to catch his breath. She heard the crunch of bone and watched as James's head snapped back. He dropped to his knees and the bell rang.

MacAvoy picked him up and carried James to his corner, grabbing a length of toweling to wipe his face. Mr. Pendergast stood beside her, cupped his hands around his mouth, and shouted, "Thirty minutes."

MacAvoy held James's limp face in his hands while the other man gave him water. She could hear MacAvoy screaming at James. "Take a knee before you're hurt worse."

James shook his head and turned out of MacAvoy's embrace when the bell rang, lurching to the center of the ring. His opponent did not look much better. MacAvoy hurried in front of their row of benches until he caught Chambliss by the arm. She could not hear what he was saying, but she sensed MacAvoy's panic. She knew he would not be in such a state unless he was very worried for his friend's health. She touched Mr. Pendergast's arm.

"What is happening?"

"I think MacAvoy is trying to talk Chambliss into calling the fight a draw."

"A draw?"

"No winner, but no loser either. He's got to get James out of that ring."

She looked back at the fighters as Chambliss made his way to the other corner. James was still swinging, barely on his feet, sweat dripping from his hair when he shook his head as if trying to clear his thoughts. She felt tears burn at the back of her eyes. She couldn't take much more of this torture!

James swung his arm, barely touching Jackson's chin but whirling the man in a circle as James's knees buckled. Both men went down as Chambliss rang the bell and shouted, "Draw! All bets hold until the rematch!"

"A rematch?" Lucinda said but then focused on MacAvoy kneeling beside James, tapping his cheek and calling his name.

She stood then, shaking free of Mr. Pendergast's hand on her elbow, pushing her way through the men crowding the ring. She bent down and stepped through the ropes, dragging her skirts behind her, nearly tripping on her petticoats. She dropped to her knees beside James.

MacAvoy was shaking his shoulders lightly and pressing a cloth to a long cut over his eye, trying to stem the flow of blood. James coughed and started to choke, but his eyes still did not open. MacAvoy reached into his mouth and pulled out a large bloody wad of fabric and then rolled him on his side.

"If he vomits, I don't want him choking on it if he hasn't woken up."

"How long? How long until he wakes up?"

He shook his head. "Don't know. I don't know if he can hear me."

"Perhaps he can hear me," Lucinda said and looked down at him, so still and bloody. She leaned over his ear. "James. James, it's Lucinda. You must wake up now. We must get your injuries tended, and we can't do it here. James? Do you hear me?"

She grabbed his hand and realized his little finger was dangling unnaturally. She took a deep breath and gripped the rest of his hand in both of hers. "James. Won't you please open your eyes?" She kissed his knuckles, dirty and bleeding, and realized she was trembling.

James coughed and then spit onto the floor. "Must be dreaming," he mumbled.

MacAvoy heaved a breath and wiped his eyes. "Why's that, you stubborn man?"

"Heard . . . Lucinda."

"You did," she cried and leaned over him. "You must never do anything this foolish ever again. Do you hear me? I will not stand for it."

His eyes fluttered. "Must be dreaming."

MacAvoy stood and motioned to Mr. Pendergast and his father. He looked at the son. "You and I are going to carry him out of here. I don't think he can walk. We're going to cross our hands and make a seat. Your father and your uncle are going to have to get him up and in our arms."

Mr. Pendergast helped her to her feet and then turned to their task. James moaned as the elder Pendergasts pulled him up by his arms.

"Pettigrew!" MacAvoy shouted. "Where's his coat?"

The man shrugged and hurried to the door. Lucinda pulled her cloak from her shoulders and wrapped it around James's body. The two men picked him up under his arms and moved him back toward where Mr. Pendergast and MacAvoy knelt and crossed their hands.

The two men got to their feet with James between them and Mr. Pendergast's father at James's back, holding him in place. She turned when the other man, Mr. Pendergast's uncle, put his hand on her elbow.

"Miss Vermeal, take my coat," he said, working to shrug out of his.

"No. No, thank you," she said, glancing at the men making slow progress out of the ring where Chambliss's men had let loose the ropes.

"Then at least take my arm. How did you arrive?"

"I have a reliable man waiting for me with a carriage, Mr. Pendergast."

"I was just getting ready to come inside for you, miss," Michael said to Lucinda as she stepped out the door.

"I'm fine, Michael. Thank you so much for waiting for me. I don't wish to go home just yet, though. I'd like to go to the Thompson home." She looked at Mr. Pendergast. "What is his address? Do you know it?"

"Number 75 Locust Street," he said after some hesitation.

"I know the area, miss," Michael said and helped her climb into the carriage. He pulled a blanket out from under the seat and handed it to her.

CHAPTER 11

Lucinda stepped out of the carriage near the Thompson home and turned to Michael. "Will you wait again?"

"Of course. My cousin would never speak to me again if I did not make sure you arrived home safely."

She walked down the street to the steps of 75 Locust Street, the light from inside the house flooding the stoop and the gas streetlights shining on several women in the doorway and carriages in front of the house. Muireall, the eldest, was directing everyone. Elspeth, Mr. Pendergast's wife, was wringing her hands and calling to her husband.

"I will tell you the whole story, but please come outside and escort Miss Vermeal into the house. She must be freezing."

"Miss Vermeal?" Mrs. Pendergast searched the street. "There you are," she said and hurried past the men. "Come inside out of the weather. Where is your coat?"

"What is this around him, MacAvoy?" Lucinda heard the old aunt say. "It looks like a woman's cape."

"It is, Aunt Murdoch," Mr. Pendergast said. "I'll tell you everything, but James needs attention now."

The aunt hurried away from the door, shouting to someone in the hall to bring toweling, hot water, and her medicine box.

Lucinda climbed the steps holding onto Mrs. Pendergast's arm. She was led into a large well-furnished room where one young man carried in a tea tray and the other, James's brother, carried in a tray of sandwiches and cake. He walked over to her when he realized who she was.

"Were you there, Miss Vermeal? What happened?"

She swallowed and looked away, suddenly overcome with emotion and chilled to the bone. The younger sister, Kirsty, hurried to her.

"You've had a fright, haven't you? Sit down. I will pour you tea. Payden, get Muireall's shawl laying there by the bookshelf."

"It was awful," she said and looked up at them. "They wouldn't stop fighting. It went over thirty minutes."

"Thirty minutes?" the brother whispered. "That's not possible."

"Do you think she's making this up?" Miss Thompson said and smacked her brother on the arm. "Look at her. Her face is pure white."

Lucinda took the cup and saucer, the china rattling in her hands. She managed a sip and sighed. She turned when she heard her name.

"You must come with me, Miss Vermeal," MacAvoy said from the doorway.

"Come where?"

"James will not settle down. He wants to see you."

"Oh." She quickly stood, setting her tea on a side table and hurrying to the door. "Oh. I must go, then."

She followed MacAvoy up the staircase, down a wide hallway, and past closed doors to one standing open. Those already inside backed away when she entered. James was shouting, although it was unintelligible as she hurried to the four-poster bed.

"James," she said and picked up his hand. "James. It's me. Lucinda."

He took a breath and smiled as much as he could with one side of his face. "Can smell you."

She pulled a chair close to his bed. "You must allow your aunt and sisters to tend you, James. You must stop fighting. You are home in your own room."

He turned his head and faced her, though his eyes were nearly swollen shut. "Lucinda."

"Yes. I am here. Now let the ladies do their work."

He nodded and accepted the liquid his aunt gave to him from a small cup. She laid his head back on the pillow and began giving brisk orders. "You must leave, Miss Vermeal. MacAvoy and I are going to peel off his pants. Out. Muireall and Elspeth too. It's unseemly to see your brother in his drawers."

Everyone left but MacAvoy, Lucinda, and the aunt. "I'm not leaving, Mrs. Murdoch. I'll turn my head, but I'm not leaving until you've made him comfortable."

Mrs. Murdoch eyed her. "Is that so? You're a society miss. What's your interest in my nephew?"

Lucinda tilted her chin. "My interest . . . my interest is none of your concern."

The aunt harrumphed and shook her head. "I always knew he would fall hard when he fell."

Once James had been stripped of his pants and covered with a sheet from his waist down, Lucinda reseated herself beside him.

"May I use this water to clean off the blood, Mrs. Murdoch?" she asked.

"Yes. I'll get more when its dirtied. There are towels beside the basin. Here, MacAvoy. Hold this needle." She looked up at Lucinda after snipping off a length of thread. "You'd best call me Aunt Murdoch, girl."

"That would be far too familiar," Lucinda said. "I wouldn't wish to insult you."

"Insult me? You're daft! Call me Aunt Murdoch, or you *will* insult me." She chuckled to herself.

Aunt Murdoch threaded the needle and knotted the end. Lucinda was not sure if she could watch the woman stitch his skin, but she took a deep breath and forced herself to glance occasionally to where she pulled the cut together and pierced each side with a needle, taking her time and making the stitches small and even.

"Don't hum while you're stitching him," MacAvoy said. "It reminds of when Mrs. McClintok sews up the stuffing in the goose for Christmas dinner."

"Does he need a doctor?" Lucinda asked.

"He might," Aunt Murdoch said. "Depends how many of his ribs are broken and if his brain is rattled beyond repair."

"Christ, Murdoch," MacAvoy said as she worked her way down James's side, feeling his ribs and eliciting startled cries from him.

"Tell Muireall to get the doctor," she said.

MacAvoy opened the door and found Payden Thompson and the other young man leaning against the wall opposite James's room. "Tell Muireall to get the doctor."

Lucinda could hear the young men jump up and clatter down the steps. A few moments later, Muireall Thompson came into the room. "I've already checked. Dr. Maxwell is delivering twins on the other side of town. He could not be here until tomorrow afternoon at the earliest."

Lucinda rose. "May I have paper and pen?"

Muireall went to the desk in the corner of James's room, opened a drawer, and pulled down the front of the desk. "Here," she said and laid paper and a pencil on the felt.

Lucinda sat down and wrote a note, folded it, and handed it to Muireall. "I need to get this note to Dr. Clay Gibson at the Medical School. He is our family physician."

"You've just moved here from Virginia. How long have you

known him that he will climb out of his bed near midnight and see a patient he's never seen before?" Muireall asked as she eyed the paper.

"My father agreed to finance a new surgical ward at the hospital. The doctor's address is on the front. He will come."

Muireall lifted one eyebrow and turned to the doorway. "Boys, find me a cab or a carriage. I'll go right away."

"At this time of night, Muireall? Let me go," MacAvoy said.

"I've got a carriage I hired out front in the street. He is reliable. Let me see if he will go," Lucinda said.

"Michael Laurent?" Muireall asked. "He's in the kitchen, having just finished a meal. It was too cold to let him stand outside."

"Oh dear! I hadn't thought of that. Thank you," she said.

"Payden, show Miss Vermeal to the kitchen so she may speak to her driver."

Lucinda gave Michael the note after he said he would convey the doctor to Locust Street if the man wished. Lucinda thanked him and was talked into sitting down at the kitchen table and having a sweet roll, fresh from the oven, by the Thompson housekeeper, Mrs. McClintok. She drank tea and ate, all the while listening to the lilting talk of the woman about inconsequential things. She'd never eaten in a kitchen before and decided she may like it. She liked the big, scarred tabletop where she sat and where Mrs. McClintok was cutting vegetables at the other end and then dropping them into a large pot on a modern stove.

"He's going to need broth when he wakes up. He always does, especially if he's loosened a tooth. He loves my chicken soup." She smiled as she stirred.

Lucinda climbed the steps to James's room and opened the door. He was thrashing on the bed, and MacAvoy and the eldest Miss Thompson were trying, unsuccessfully, to hold him still while Aunt Murdoch applied an ointment to cuts on his hand. She hurried to his bedside.

"James," she said and ran her fingers over his forehead. "James. Lie still so your aunt can help you."

"Lucinda?" he whispered.

"I'm here, James." She sat down beside his bed. "Lie still. You'll injure yourself more than you already are." He reached out blindly for her, and she took his hand. "I'm here."

"Dr. Gibson is here, Muireall," Elspeth said after opening the door.

"Bring him up, please."

Dr. Gibson entered the room, looking a bit rumpled and somewhat confused. "Miss Vermeal?"

She stood and went straight to him. "Doctor, thank you so much for coming."

He glanced over her shoulder. "This is the patient, I take it?"

"Lucinda?" James said and moaned.

She hurried to his bed. "James. The doctor is here. You must allow him to examine you."

He moved his head from side to side. His breathing shallow. "Lucinda."

"Dr. Gibson? Can you help him?"

The doctor eyed her for a long moment and then went to the other side of the bed. "This is James Thompson? The bareknuckle fighter?" He bent down and examined the stitches over James's eye. "Who's responsible for these stitches?"

"Mrs. Murdoch beside you, Doctor. She is the one who thought we'd best call a doctor. She is concerned about his ribs."

The doctor turned to Aunt Murdoch. "That's fine stitching, ma'am. Perhaps you'd like to come and teach some of my students."

Aunt Murdoch harrumphed and then reached around to touch James's side. "I think he's got several broken ribs, but I'm worried about this one." She touched the spot. "I'm worried he's punctured his lung."

The doctor glanced down at her. "What else have you observed?"

"I dosed him with some brandy laced with just a bit of the poppy. I didn't want to give too much because I'm worried his head, although as hard as a hundred-year-old brick, has been beaten so much his brain is scrambled. For the cuts on his hands and lips, I've used an aloe salve I make especially for him. The little finger on his left hand is broken in several places. I was just thinking about what I could use for a splint."

"I'm going to examine his ribs, and he's not going to like it," the doctor said. "I'd like to wash my hands."

The doctor was back shortly and had MacAvoy lift James to a sitting position while he listened to his chest with an instrument that fit in his ears at one end with a tube attached that ended with a funnel-shaped piece of rubber. He asked everyone to be quiet while he listened to James's chest.

"What do you think?" Aunt Murdoch asked.

"I don't think it is punctured, but it is severely irritated. His heart sounds strong, although I think he's lost a good bit of blood. I don't believe in the antiquated practice of bloodletting. We'll need to restore blood, which his body will produce. He needs considerable rest."

"Thank God," Aunt Murdoch murmured.

"As to if his brain is 'scrambled,' we'll have to wait and see how he is when he wakes up fully. I know he's in pain, but I do not recommend anything other than willow bark tea. Apply ice to his eyes and face three times a day to reduce the swelling and keep him in bed. He's got to give his body time to heal. Now let's get that finger set. He's going to howl when I straighten the bone, so if anyone cares to leave the room, do so now. Mrs. Murdoch, what have you decided we should use as a splint?"

Aunt Murdoch and the doctor moved to her side of James's bed, as they talked and examined what Aunt Murdoch had pulled out of her apron pocket.

"Can you step to the other side of the bed, Miss Vermeal?"

She stood and laid James's hand down beside him. He began to move on the bed, trying to sit up or roll over. MacAvoy held him down by the shoulders as the doctor was trying to hold his hand still.

"My God, this man is strong," he said.

"Don't ever get hit by him, Doc," MacAvoy said. "My jaw hurt for a month."

"This isn't going to work," Doctor Gibson said, watching James struggle.

"He was fine while I held his hand," she said. "Let me hold his hand while you set it."

"You could try holding his other hand."

Lucinda shook her head. "No. I'd prefer to hold his hand while you straighten that finger."

"Are you sure?" the doctor asked.

She nodded. "Tell me what to do."

The doctor had MacAvoy squeeze beside her to hold James's shoulder while she held his hand in place and talked softly to him. James moaned and quivered as the doctor probed his finger.

"Three, two, one."

Lucinda doubted she would ever forget the sounds the bones made as the doctor wedged them into place. James shouted once and then fainted, something she was in danger of doing herself. But she could not. She could not stop supporting his hand and holding it still so the doctor and Aunt Murdoch could continue. She let out a held breath when the doctor stepped back after tying off the strips of linen holding the wooden supports together. She was suddenly exhausted.

"I'll sit with him," MacAvoy said.

Muireall handed him a blanket and a pillow and turned to Lucinda. "Would you like to stay here?"

She shook her head. "No. I must get home, but I can wait until Michael takes the doctor home."

"I came in my own gig. Take the carriage home and get some sleep," the doctor said as he pulled on his coat. "Does your father know you are here?"

She shook her head. "He does not."

"And you would prefer I keep this between the two of us, I imagine."

"Do as you must, Dr. Gibson. Your actions are not in my control."

He smiled at her. "No, they are not. But I'm feeling a lapse of memory coming on. Good night all. I'll send my bill to this address."

Muireall led the doctor out the door, and Lucinda turned to MacAvoy. "You will watch over him?"

"I will."

"You will get a message to me if he worsens?"

He nodded. "Yes. Now go home and get some rest."

"Thank you for stopping that match. You saved his life, I think."

"We've saved each other's over the years. But I'm glad the fight stopped when it did."

CHAPTER 12

James woke up slowly, licking his lip where the skin was split. He could feel a scab forming and tasted the foul salve that Aunt Murdoch made for his cuts. He was home, in his room; he could see through the slit available to him on his right eye. He bent his elbow, bringing his hand into view, touching his face gingerly. Swollen lips and a long row of neat stitches above his left eye.

"Awake, are you?" he heard from the side of his bed. It was Muireall's voice.

"Thirsty."

She leaned over him, holding up his head, which pounded like the devil, and touching his lips to a glass. He took a long, steady drink and laid his head back on the pillow.

"Do you know your name?"

"What?"

"Your name. Do you know your name and where you are?"

"Hell, Muireall," he stuttered, slobbering down his chin. "If I'm not in my own bed on Locust Street, I've gone to hell, where elder sisters jab at a man when he's down."

He took a breath and closed his eye, as that muttering had exhausted him.

"Your name?"

"James Bryan Burns Thompson," he whispered.

"Aunt Murdoch will be glad to hear your brains aren't scrambled."

He rumbled a laugh but immediately winced in pain and clutched his side. "Jesus, Mary, and all the Saints. That hurts."

"Nothing less than you deserve," she said and walked out of the room.

Aunt Murdoch tapped his shoulder. "Probably the only thing on you that doesn't hurt."

"Tell me."

"I'll tell you after you've let go of your water. Payden's going to help you," she said.

Payden came into view. "Aunt Murdoch told me to help you sit up, get to the edge of the bed, and take a piss. But I ain't touching your peter."

James eyed his brother, who was grimacing. "Just get me to the edge of the bed, boy. Far enough I don't piss down the quilt, or Aunt Murdoch will be in here watching me."

Payden shook his head. "A piss is a man's private business. Can you wrap your arms around my neck?"

James did as he was told and groaned when Payden jerked him up. "Easy!"

Payden swung James's legs over the side of the bed and tucked the blanket and sheets under the mattress. "Can you get your ass forward?"

James inched forward, feeling dizzy and nauseous. "Don't let me fall. Don't have my bearings."

Payden held his shoulders while he fumbled with his drawers, eventually leaning his head against Payden's chest.

"Your piss is bloody, and there's three day's worth in that pot."

"What day is it?"

"Tuesday."

"When did I fight Jackson?"

"Saturday."

"Did I win?"

Payden laughed. "Not quite."

James closed his eye and tried to remember what had happened, but all he saw were flashes. Flickers of light and color and MacAvoy's face. He could see Jackson's fist coming at him, feel himself block the punch or shift out of the way, and it made him a little sick suddenly remembering the connection of knuckles to chin and the snap of his neck as he withstood the blow. And there was a scent that remained in his head aside from the stink of sweat and sawdust. Roses. He'd smelled roses.

"Payden? Is he decent?"

"Aunt Murdoch is calling," Payden said and looked down. "Are you done?"

James nodded and let Payden ease him back onto the pillows. He'd been laid up for a day or two from a fight before, a few days when Padino had punched him in the throat with coins wrapped in his palm. But never like this. He'd never been . . . incapacitated.

* * *

"Carlton Young and his papa are due to arrive day after tomorrow," Lucinda's father said as the first course of their luncheon was served.

A servant placed a warm yeast roll on her plate. It made her think of that sweet roll she'd had in the Thompsons' kitchen the night of James's bout. She wondered how he was doing, if he'd recovered from his injuries. She'd not slept that night after tapping on the wall of Aunt Louisa's room. She could not stop envisioning his battered face, the pull of the thread as Aunt Murdoch stitched him, and that sound, oh dear, that sound when the doctor straightened his finger.

"How lovely," she said and tasted her soup.

"You'd best be on good behavior, Daughter. Carlton is a perfect match for this family."

"But he may not be a perfect match for Lucinda, Henri," Aunt Louisa said.

The meal continued, her father's edicts becoming more strident and Aunt's objections more vocal. She was glad to not be involved. She had no intentions of marrying Carlton Young, but she did not care to discuss that decision just now. Aunt had just stood when Laurent came into the dining room.

"Pardon me," he said with a deferential nod to her father. "There are callers here for Miss Lucinda and Miss Vermeal. Would you like me to show them to the yellow salon?"

"Callers?" Father asked.

"Yes, Henri. Callers," Aunt Louisa said. "We do occasionally have guests. The yellow salon is fine, Laurent. Please send a tray with coffee and tea."

Lucinda and her aunt made their way to the salon, and a servant opened the door as the tea cart was being wheeled inside.

"Miss Thompson and Mrs. Pendergast! How delightful. I have not seen you since your lovely party at the Pendergasts' last month," Aunt Louisa said.

Lucinda's heart began to race. Why were they here? Had they come to deliver terrible news? She was rooted to the entrance of the room and felt the blood drain from her face. Mrs. Pendergast hurried toward her.

"Do not make yourself uneasy. James is recovering," she said quietly.

Lucinda let out a held breath and fought for composure. She closed her eyes briefly.

"Thank you, Mrs. Pendergast."

"What a lovely tea service," she said and led Lucinda to a chair.

Aunt Louisa poured tea for everyone, and Lucinda was glad to see she could accept the china without her hand shaking noticeably. They talked for several minutes about inconsequential everyday things. Lucinda wondered if they'd not said anything more about James because her aunt was in the room.

"The real reason we've come to see you, other than enjoying this chat and this fine tea," Mrs. Pendergast said, "is to invite you to a luncheon."

"I do some charity work for a catholic orphanage in our neighborhood," Muireall Thompson said. "We'll be having our annual bazaar next month, and one of the items for sale will be a handmade quilt we've been working on. Because of some excitement in our family, we've fallen behind. We thought we might enlist you to join us to help quilt and to have a meal."

Lucinda looked up as her father came into the room. "Ladies." He nodded. "Welcome to our home."

"We were just asking the Misses Vermeal if they would join us for a charitable undertaking," Mrs. Pendergast said.

"A charitable undertaking? Will a donation be helpful?"

"Donations are always appreciated at the Sisters of Charity Orphanage. But this is more a request for their skilled labor," Miss Thompson said.

"Of course, of course. Get the address, Louisa. We'll send something within the month. Afternoon, ladies," he said as he turned to leave.

Lucinda waited until she heard the door close. "I would be happy to help."

"Where will we be stitching this quilt?" Aunt Louisa asked. "At the orphanage?"

Muireall Thompson looked directly at Lucinda. "75 Locust Street. We hope you both could join us in the afternoon and plan on staying for your evening meal."

Aunt glanced at her. "We would be delighted. What day were you planning?"

"Tomorrow, if your schedules suit. The quilt is . . . impatiently waiting," Mrs. Pendergast said.

"That would be best," Aunt said. "My brother has invited guests to stay for a few days, and Lucinda and I are to entertain the son of that family. They are to arrive day after tomorrow."

Mrs. Pendergast glanced her way. "Then tomorrow it is. And I do think we should do away with all the formality. I am Elspeth. My sisters are Muireall and Kirsty, and my brothers are James and Payden."

"Of course," Aunt said. "I am Louisa, and my niece is Lucinda."

"We must be going. Thank you very much for the tea and conversation. We will see you tomorrow, then?" Elspeth asked as she and her sister rose.

"Yes," Lucinda said. "I am very much looking forward to it."

They watched the two women climb into the Pendergast carriage with help from their coachman. "What lovely ladies," Aunt said. "And I am very happy to be involved in some more charitable work, having left behind all of my committees in Virginia."

"It will be an enjoyable afternoon."

"Will it, Lucinda?" Aunt said with a wry smile. "And what part will be the most enjoyable?"

"I'm sure it will all be quite lovely."

* * *

JAMES LEANED HEAVILY ON PAYDEN AS HE MADE HIS WAY DOWN the steps of the Thompson house. "My God. I feel as if I'm a hundred years old."

"Then why are you leaving your bed, James? You've got everyone fussing over you and waiting on you. Even Muireall hurries to get the next thing you need."

"I'm going out of my mind laying up there in bed. Got to see some walls that aren't the ones I've been staring at for a week."

James was in plain pants and a homespun shirt, his thick robe over it all. He couldn't bring himself to bend down to pull on a boot or a shoe, as his head pounded when he leaned over. He made his way into the parlor and found all but two chairs in front of the wide front window.

"Redecorating, are we?" he said to no one in particular as Payden led him to the large chair still in its place close to the fire that was roaring. He sat and propped his stocking feet up on the hassock that Payden was pushing his way.

Elspeth looked up from what she was working on. "We're quilting and need the light."

"And all the chairs?" he asked. Not that he cared, but it was good to be discussing something other than the thickness of his scabs and the color of his piss.

"We're having company," Muireall said, glancing at the mantel clock. "They should be here any moment."

"Damn it to hell, Muireall. Why didn't you tell me? Come here, Payden. Help me into the kitchen."

The knock on the front door got James to his feet without help. He had no intention of allowing anyone other than family to see his pitiful self. He was holding on to the back of his chair, readying himself to walk through the dining room, when he heard her voice.

"How kind you are to invite us. I've been so looking forward to it."

"To quilting?" Kirsty asked.

"Yes. Yes, to quilting and to renewing friendships."

He turned then and saw her at the door. Her dress a pale blue with some intricate lace collar the color of her hair, which was piled loosely on her head. She was neither smiling nor frowning, as was her usual serene look, her posture erect. She looked like a princess or a queen, and she was walking straight toward him. Every other thing around him fell away from his vision, leaving him to focus on her until she was just a few feet away.

"Sit down, James," she said. "You're swaying on your feet. Didn't your sisters tell you I would be visiting with my aunt?"

He limped around the side of the chair, holding the arm, until he was in front of the chair. He looked up at her, hoping she would seat herself before he fell over and hit his head on the hearth. She sat while his sisters enveloped her aunt, guiding her to the settee facing the window. It was then he noticed the quilting frame in the middle of the seats.

He eased himself into the chair and leaned back, winded with just that small amount of movement. Why was she here? "Lucinda?"

"Yes, James?"

He licked his lips and pulled out his handkerchief to dab his lip. Even though the swelling was mostly down, the cuts there were still healing. "Why have you come here?" he asked and stared into the fire.

"Perhaps I am waiting to hear your thanks for awakening you while you lay on that filthy floor of the boxing ring or for wiping the blood from your face while your aunt sewed your skin together. Maybe I'm hoping to hear how your hand is healing after holding it still so the doctor could set the bone. Maybe that is why I am here."

She was spitting mad, but another person would not know that from the tone of her voice or the expression on her face. She sounded as serene as if thanking a servant for a glass of wine. But he could tell she was furious. Her eyes gave it away. And then he thought about what she'd said. He leaned forward in his chair.

"Are you saying you were at the match?"

"Yes. I was at the match. At the end . . . at the end, when MacAvoy could not wake you, I held your hand and called your name."

"What is the matter with you? A fight is no place for a gentle-woman. Good Lord! There are drunks and rowdy—"

"I was there. I went home safely."

She had been at the Jackson fight; she had seen him humiliated. She had seen him beaten. "And you're waiting for my thanks? You'll be sitting there for a long time."

"You are on your dignity, are you not?"

"On my dignity! Good God, woman. I have no dignity. Look at me, just look at me," he whispered furiously.

"I am looking at you, James."

"I'm nothing. I've got nothing. I'll never *be* anything."

He could have cried, having voiced those fears, especially to her. The most beautiful, desirable woman he'd ever met. He looked away so that she would not see the pain in his eyes. She reached down and picked up her little bag and opened it. Peering inside, she pulled out a book.

"I thought I'd read a bit to you from *Pride and Prejudice*. It's a favorite book of mine."

"You're going to read to me?"

"Yes. Please get comfortable and put your feet up here," she said and pushed the hassock under his legs.

She began reading, and to his dismay, he could not stop her. Did not want to stop her. Listening to her soft, aristocratic voice let him relax. He laid his head back against the chair and stared at the fire.

LUCINDA READ THE FIRST CHAPTER AND GLANCED UP TO SEE James had fallen asleep. She took the plaid blanket from the back of her chair and laid it across him. His eyes were no longer swollen shut, but the skin around them was bruised and turning various shades of yellow. The stitched cut seemed to be healing nicely. She turned and went to the window where the women were stitching at a large quilt.

"How is Mr. Thompson?" Aunt Louisa asked as she was seated.

"He is sleeping," she said and pulled a needle from the pincushion.

Aunt Louisa chuckled. "I realize that. I was wondering how he was feeling."

"He's tired and weak right now. And not in the mood to talk, although he did listen as I read." She noticed Muireall staring at her.

"His body continues to heal," Muireall said as she eyed the stitches she'd made and then glanced at Lucinda.

"He's bored now, as he heals, and maybe feeling a little blue-deviled," Elspeth said.

His sisters were aware of his mood as well, it seemed, even if their remarks were subtle.

"He's more than a little blue-deviled," Kirsty said. "He's not himself. He's melancholy, I think."

Lucinda glanced at him, thankfully still sleeping soundly, as she believed he would be angry to hear them talk about him. "Has MacAvoy been to visit him?"

"Last time MacAvoy came by, James told me to tell him he was sleeping," Muireall said.

"I am so worried about him. And Alexander blames himself," Elspeth said.

"I'd like to shake that boy until his brains rattle," Aunt Murdoch said. "I've been sewing him back together and binding his ribs since he left off his short pants. He was strong even as a young boy and got himself into scrapes in the old country too."

"I had hoped to speak to him before his bout, but I was not able to. And we have guests coming tomorrow, and I'll be unable to visit for at least a few days," Lucinda said as she rose. "I am going to help him upstairs to his room. I'd like to stay and speak to him, if he'll allow it."

Aunt Louisa studied her needle. "Do what you think is best, dear."

James was beginning to stir when she got to his chair. "Will you allow me to help you up to your room?"

He looked up at her, and she thought he might argue, but then he took a deep breath and put both hands on the arms of the chair. He stood, wobbling a bit, but walked toward the door of the sitting room.

"May I help you up the stairs?" Robbie McClintok asked as they walked slowly into the hallway.

James put a hand on the newel post. "I'm fine, son. Thank you."

Lucinda climbed the stairs, one step behind him. He stood very still at the top of the steps, she thought to catch his breath, before continuing to his room. "You shouldn't be up here with me, girl."

"Your sisters and both of our aunts know where I am going."

He sat down on the side of his bed after Lucinda helped him off with his robe. She propped the pillows against the headboard and laid a blanket over him.

"Would you like to finish your nap?" she asked.

"You should leave."

"I'd like to talk to you for a few minutes, and then I will leave."

He crossed his arms over his chest. "Talk."

"I don't know if you remember, but I was here the night of the match. I was because I'd wrapped you in my cape, and your sister Kirsty put a shawl around my shoulders and gave me a cup of tea. I'd only taken a sip when MacAvoy told me I had to come to your room. They could not get you to settle down long enough to tend you. I sat by your side while the doctor examined you, while they set your finger, while Aunt Murdoch stitched that cut over your eye."

James looked at her. "Why did you stay?"

"I watched you fight. I was terrified and horrified too. I'd never seen anything so violent in my life," she continued as if he had not spoken. "I was sick to my stomach with worry and revulsion. And I wondered why anyone would subject themselves to a fight like that and why anyone would care to see it. But the truth of the matter is that you were magnificent. Even tired, there was an elegance in how you moved and the power you wielded. You were prepared and diligent and ferocious. You never gave up, although I am so happy that Chambliss called a draw and it ended."

James shrugged and looked out the window. "I wasn't as prepared as I should have been. Jackson was the best fighter I ever faced."

"Why don't you think you were prepared?"

He was silent for a few long moments and then faced her. "I fired MacAvoy. I should have never done it. It was stupid and prideful. He's the best cornerman and trainer there is. What a fool I was."

"Please get well, James. There are people who care deeply for you," she said as she stood.

He hitched one side of his mouth up, reminding her what a devastatingly attractive man he was. "And are you one of them, Miss Vermeal?"

She lifted one brow and went to the door. "Get your rest, Mr. Thompson."

CHAPTER 13

"What do you need, Muireall?" MacAvoy said, coming through the kitchen door amid a whirl of snow.

"It was James who asked I send that message to you. He's in his room," she said and continued examining the shelves of the pantry beside the kitchen.

It had been six weeks since the bout with Jackson, and he'd not heard a peep from his very best friend. He was saddened by it to a degree he had not expected. He knocked on James's door and heard a muffled "enter." What he saw shocked him. James was on the floor of his room, bare to the waist, stretched out on his toes, pushing himself up off the floor with his arms—and every fifth one with just one arm. Sweat was dripping off of him. He jumped to his feet and pulled a towel around his neck.

"MacAvoy."

"You're feeling better, are you?"

"Much. Ribs are healed. Hand is healed. My head is clear. I've been training for the last two weeks. It was a slog the first few days, but I'm getting back in shape."

MacAvoy turned his hat in his hands. "I'm glad to hear it, James."

James looked down at his bare feet. This was the part that was going to be particularly hard for him as he had little experience with being contrite or regretful. But he had to do it. If he was ever to box again, he needed MacAvoy, and he needed him regardless. He'd not seen his best friend for nearly two months.

"The thing is, Malcolm, I fucked up." He continued when he saw MacAvoy smile. "I should have never fired you. You're the best cornerman in the business, and I was foolish and full of myself to think I'd done what I'd done in the ring alone. You are as much a part of my success as my fives. I couldn't have done any of it without you."

"I just didn't understand why, James. You're my best friend. I want you to stand with me when I marry Mrs. Emory."

"Is it enough for me to tell you I'm a horse's arse?"

MacAvoy shrugged. "It's factual anyway."

James laughed and held out his hand. "Are we good?"

"Yes. We're good," MacAvoy said and shook James's hand. "Why are you working out in your bedroom? Why not at one of the rings? And what are you working out for?"

"What do you think?"

MacAvoy shook his head. "No. Don't tell me you're going back in the ring."

James nodded slowly. "I have to. I have to finish it."

"No, you don't. You don't have to finish anything. You're the champ."

"It was a draw, MacAvoy. There's to be a rematch. And you have to get me ready to fight."

MacAvoy backed up, holding his hands in front of him. "And risk Murdoch's wrath, let alone your sisters'? Even Payden would be pissed. We almost lost you, James."

"You're not going to lose me, but I am going to beat Jackson in the ring. It will be my last fight, I promise."

"It damn well may be your last fight if you don't have a decent cornerman."

"Exactly."

"One thing, though, James, and you're not going to like it. You've got to do what I tell you during the fight. If I tell you to take a knee, you've got to do it. You've got to listen to me. I won't do it otherwise."

"I never had to take a knee before."

"But Jackson is different than any other boxer you've faced. You know it. If you fight him, you're going to have to be clever about it. You can't just go out in the ring like you've done so many times and clobber the other boxer with overwhelming strength. He's as strong as you, but he has weaknesses too. I'll not do it unless you promise me."

James took a deep breath. He hated the idea of stopping the match, but he knew in his heart that MacAvoy was right, that Jackson was near his equal, and if he didn't use his strength judiciously, he'd end up on his back—or dead, as MacAvoy implied. "I promise."

* * *

"THE YOUNG FAMILY IS COMING TO THE CITY, RENTING A house, and planning on an extended stay," Lucinda's father said over dinner.

"How nice." Aunt Louisa turned to her. "I'd like to visit Madame LaFray's this week, dear. Now that Renaldo's family is here permanently, I thought I might take Susannah for some new dresses, and she is very excited to go. Without her older sister nearby, she's had to rely on her papa. He has excellent taste, of course, but he does not know what clothing would please a twelve-year-old girl. Would you like to come too? It will be such fun!"

"I thought we might host a ball," her father said.

"A ball, Henri? For any particular occasion?"

He laid down his silverware and looked at Aunt Louisa. "I just told you. The Youngs are coming to Philadelphia, and I thought we could introduce them to Philadelphia society, as it were."

"I will not be sponsoring Mrs. Althea Young in any way into Philadelphia society. She is a social climber and an unpleasant woman as well. Do as you want, Henri, but I won't attend," she said.

"Not attend? Wouldn't it be a good time to introduce Delgado as well?"

Aunt Louisa stilled. "Yes. It would be a very good time to introduce Renaldo and his family." She took a deep breath. "But I will have a party here for their family alone or have it at whatever home he settles on, if you'd rather I didn't go to the expense separately."

He signaled for more wine and turned to Lucinda. "It sounds as though your aunt may be busy. Why don't you take charge of this event, my dear? Your very first ball to plan all on your own. Spare no expense either, Daughter. I don't want the Youngs to think we've cheaped on our entertainments."

"Thank you for your confidence in me, Papa, but I really have no interest in planning an event such as this," Lucinda said.

"Come now," he said. "You'll be planning these sorts of events as a married woman. May as well begin now."

She shook her head. "I have no plans to marry at this time."

"No plans to marry? I was hoping to announce an engagement at this ball, but if you need more time to get to know him, I suppose we'll just have to announce it in the papers, although I find that practice gauche."

Aunt opened her mouth to speak, but Lucinda stopped her. "Papa," she said and waited until he looked at her. "I have no plans to marry at this time, and I can tell you, with certainty, I never intend to marry Carlton Young."

"Lucinda," he said, his voice rising.

"Papa," she spoke over his words. "I will never marry Carlton Young. There is no more to discuss on the subject." She rose from her chair and laid her linen napkin beside her plate. "I've lost my appetite."

Lucinda slowly climbed the steps to her room. She was sure that at sometime in the future, she would have to accept that she may be separating herself permanently from her father. She recognized his single-mindedness on the subject of marriage for her and knew that he would not relent. That he would continue his campaign until she took an irretrievable step. Her aunt followed her to her bedroom.

Lucinda closed the door behind Aunt Louisa. "Mr. Delgado is buying a house in Philadelphia?"

"Yes. He's had an agent searching ever since he sailed back to Spain to close up his offices and sell his home there."

"Do you think you'll be joining him in his new house?"

Aunt Louisa blushed. "Renaldo has proposed, and I have accepted, although we won't be married until you are settled. Don't worry about that."

"Would he consider allowing me to reside with his family, with you, once you are married?"

Aunt rushed to her and held her hands. "There is nothing that would give me greater joy, but I worry that it may cause a permanent rift between you and your father. When did you begin thinking about this?"

"I'm almost twenty-five. Truthfully, I don't really want to join your and Mr. Delgado's household, although I think the both of you would make it very comfortable for me." She looked up at her aunt with a wry smile. "I'm going to tell Papa that I want a home of my own. He has several properties that would be suitable. I have monies from Mother's family coming to me on my next birthday that should keep me fed and clothed with suitable servants."

Aunt Louisa dropped into a chair. "You are going to ask your father for one of these homes, and when he refuses, you're going to tell him you're moving in with Renaldo and I."

Lucinda nodded. "I am."

"You tricky girl! He will sign over a property in an instant rather than have you under Renaldo's roof."

"That is the plan." Lucinda smiled. "You are free to marry Mr. Delgado at your leisure."

* * *

"You're going to kill me, MacAvoy," James sputtered as he dragged a wagon loaded with lumber down the alley. He'd put his arms through the ropes for the horse harnesses at the front of the cart and moved forward inch by precious inch. He'd made it down the alley once and turned it, now making his way back toward number 75.

"We're going to increase your stamina, James. I want you to get to exhaustion and have the strength to go on. Think about that wagon as if it were Jackson's face. Fight through it," MacAvoy said, walking beside him.

"I'd rather . . . think of it . . . as yours. As I drag your . . . nose through this gravel," James said.

"Think of it anyway you'd like. You've not far now. I can see your back gate."

James pulled his shaking arms out of the harness and bent at his waist, taking deep breaths.

"Come on," MacAvoy said. "Let's take one walk down the alley and back. We'll be done for the day then."

"Did you talk to Chambliss?"

MacAvoy nodded. "Set for the twenty-fourth."

"After your wedding?"

"Hell yes, James. I don't want you standing at the altar beside me with two black eyes. And Elspeth has engaged someone to take pictures of us. Have you seen any of them? Of the daguerreotypes? There are pictures of the battlefields at Gettysburg at the Philadelphia Museum. Rows upon rows of dead men."

"And you're worried about me with a black eye?"

MacAvoy laughed and then sobered. "You're going to be there, right? At my wedding?"

"I'm standing up for you. Of course I'll be there."

"Every time I think about standing up in front of all those people, some of them society folk, it makes me near sick to my stomach. I keep thinking someone's going to stand up and ask why some rummy's kid thinks himself good enough to marry Eleanor Emory."

"I'm going to be right beside you. Nobody's going to say anything like that without answering to me. And anyway, it's just so much shit. You've made something of yourself, you have a new promotion at your work, and you are marrying an upright, beautiful woman. Nobody gets to say anything to you."

"And don't forget Mary. I'm going to be a papa right off," MacAvoy said with a shaking voice.

"We won't forget Mary. She'll have you wrapped around her finger before you leave the church. Is Elspeth watching her while you take Mrs. MacAvoy to Annapolis for a honeymoon?"

"Yes. Eleanor could hardly believe that her employer would do such a thing, but Mary is so excited, and your sister has all kinds of things planned for the two of them. Eleanor doesn't really have anyone else, other than an elderly aunt. Her parents are dead, and Mr. Emory's parents are still in England."

"They'll have a grand time, you know. Elspeth can hardly wait for her own wee one to be born, so this will be good practice for her," James said with a laugh.

MacAvoy stopped when they'd rounded the alley and put his hands on James's shoulders. "You've got to promise me that you will keep up with all of your workouts while I'm away."

"I will, MacAvoy. I promise. You won't be thinking about me while you're away anyway, man. Let's hope Mrs. Emory can keep you occupied."

James laughed at the look on MacAvoy's face and the blush

rising up his neck. His friend looked away with a grin. "I don't know what you're talking about."

"It's all you can think about, MacAvoy." James laughed. "I've known you since you were a boy, remember?"

"No more than you think about Miss Vermeal. Don't look at me like that," MacAvoy said. "I've seen how you look at her. You're thinking about her now."

He *was* thinking about her. He was thinking about that declaration she'd made and how he'd acted as if her words didn't affect him, making a glib comment about whether she was one of the people that cared deeply for him. But her words had affected him. He could not deny it, as he went to sleep every night hearing her words in his head and letting himself review them, steep himself in them, trying to understand why his heart pounded hard in his chest as he thought of them. *The truth of the matter is that you were magnificent. Even tired, there was an elegance in how you moved and the power you wielded.*

"Let me buy you a whiskey before the wedding. Before you're a married man who's not allowed to meet an old friend."

"Won't be a case of not being allowed, Thompson." MacAvoy laughed as he began to walk down the alley. "I'll just prefer her company to yours!"

James made his way to his rooms, his legs shaking with the effort to climb the stairs. Thankfully, the bathing room was empty. He locked the door, stripped, and climbed into a tub of very hot water, the steam rising around his face and shoulders, easing the aches in his muscles from MacAvoy's grueling training.

Clean and feeling better, he went to the parlor, hearing feminine laughter and voices. "Muireall. Kirsty. What brings you by today, Elspeth?"

"Nothing of any moment. Just missing my sisters and brothers," she said as she crossed the room and kissed his cheek. "It is so good to see you looking well."

"It is good to see you too. How are you feeling? Have you seen the doctor lately?"

"I'm feeling fine! Wonderful, in fact!"

He chuckled. "That's good. I'm to the kitchen for some of Mrs. McClintok's soup and bread. I missed luncheon."

"Have you heard the news, James? Elspeth is to have a new neighbor," Kirsty said.

"I hadn't." James glanced at Elspeth. "Hopefully no one that would cause you trouble."

"Oh no. No trouble at all! It will be nice having a friend in the neighborhood."

"A friend? Of our family?" James said with a laugh. "Moving into those big fancy homes in your neighborhood? A friend of the Pendergasts?"

"No, James. A friend of yours," Kirsty said.

"A friend of mine?"

"Miss Vermeal is moving into a home just two blocks away from ours, on Thirty-Eighth Street."

"Miss Vermeal?"

"I sent a note to her telling her to dine with us if her kitchen or staff are not ready."

"Miss Vermeal and her father have moved from that mansion they have?"

Elspeth shook her head. "I don't believe her father has moved there. From her note back to me, I believe she will live there alone."

"Alone?"

"Quit repeating everything Elspeth says," Muireall said and shook her head. "Miss Vermeal is no concern of yours. Come sit down, girls. Our coffee is getting cold."

James headed to the kitchen, not breaking his stride as he picked up the heel of the freshly baked bread Mrs. McClintok was slicing, and down the stairs to the back door. He could have waited until Elspeth was done visiting and ridden with her in the

Pendergast carriage to that neighborhood, but he preferred to catch a streetcar and see exactly what was happening right away. He jumped off the streetcar fifteen minutes later and headed south down the alley behind one side of Thirty-Eighth Street, where the larger homes were located. It did not take him long to find the house with a new mistress. All manner of wagons and carts were pulled behind the stables, where men were unloading trunks and cases and carrying them into the house. He picked up a small trunk and joined the line of workmen.

"THAT TRUNK GOES UPSTAIRS. SHOW MRS. HOWELL, STANDING there on the landing. She will tell you what room it is to go in," Lucinda said and looked up the steps. "I think these are the bedlinens I ordered, Mrs. Howell."

"Yes, miss," the woman said and pointed the men down the hallway. Lucinda turned to the next workman. She could not stop the hint of a smile when she saw who carried the trunk.

"Mr. Thompson. Are you in the moving business now?"

"I'm in the business of finding out whether this harebrained scheme of yours to live alone is true."

"Harebrained?" She raised a brow.

James glanced around at the workmen and maids coming and going. "May we speak alone, Miss Vermeal?"

"Mrs. Howell? Can you take over here for me? I think we are getting to the end of the wagons."

Lucinda turned and led James to a small room under the staircase that she planned on using as an office, where she could meet tradesmen or staff. She'd ordered a desk and rolling chair to be put by the small bookcase and a comfortable chair and hassock for in front of the fireplace. It was empty now, although it did smell of paint and wallpaper paste.

"What may I help you with, Mr. Thompson? What could you possibly—" Her words were cut off when he kissed her.

She responded immediately as he pulled her tight against him and plowed her mouth with his tongue. He groaned, and she murmured his name. Several minutes later, she pulled her face from his.

"What are you doing here, James?" Her lips were parted and her eyes soft in response to his claiming.

He moved her away from him but held her firmly by the waist.

"Is your father moving in here with you? Or your aunt?"

She shook her head. "No. Aunt Louisa will soon be married, and the entire point of setting up my own household was to escape my papa."

"I can't believe he allowed it."

She moved away from him. She had to. Her mind was scattered when he was near. "I told him I wanted to move into one of the homes he owns throughout the city, and of course, he refused. I told him then that I was moving in with Aunt Louisa and Mr. Delgado as soon as they married."

"And he was not happy about that?"

"Truthfully, I've never seen him that angry. So much of it is about his plans for me to marry Carlton Young."

"Who is Carlton Young?"

"The son of one of father's business associates. He says he is perfect for me. He'll be easily manipulated by Papa while he is alive and by me when Papa is gone."

"Does this poor chump know what he's in for?"

"Of course not. I have no intentions of marrying him."

James shook his head and held a thumb and forefinger to his temple. "You bought this house instead of marrying Young?"

"No, no. This is Papa's property. Well, it's part of the Vermeal estate. He was so furious I'd consider moving in with Mr. Delgado and Aunt that he relented and gave me the keys."

James laughed ruefully. "You remind me of a quiet Kirsty. She gets her way by hook or by crook."

"Thank you, I guess," she said.

"I don't like this, Lucinda. Not one bit."

"I don't believe you have any say in it."

"I don't?" He stalked closer.

She shook her head, working to keep her voice calm and steady. "Hardly. I'm not betrothed to you. I've not even accompanied you anywhere like the theater. I've not even seen you since I visited you on Locust Street and read to you."

"I've been busy. But I have plans for us."

"You have plans? How interesting. Were you going to apprise me of these plans?"

"At some point."

"Mr. Thompson, I do not take kindly to edicts from a man so wholly disconnected from me."

"It won't be an edict, Lucinda."

"And what have you been busy doing? Has your family's business been keeping you from these plans?"

"MacAvoy's wedding is coming up. I'm his best man," James said.

"And that has kept you so busy?"

He shrugged. "I'm training six or seven hours a day too. And there's always errands to do for the business."

"Training for what? What kind of training?" Lucinda asked, feeling a prickle of unease as she looked at him. He was not completely comfortable telling her, whatever it was. She could see it in his face.

"The rematch is set for the twenty-fourth. MacAvoy's got me in the best shape of my life. I've never worked harder."

"Rematch? What are you talking about?"

"With Jackson. The rematch with Jackson is set for two weeks from now."

Lucinda felt as if there was not enough air in the room to breathe. She shook her head, staring at him, knowing that it was not a joke and she had not misheard him. She was suddenly and completely furious, making her feel in charity with her father when he lost his temper. But she was a lady. She would not scream. Instead, she pointed to the door of the room.

"Get out," she said. "Get out and do not ever, ever set foot on this property again."

"I have every intention of—"

"I said get out. Remove yourself, you foolish man. I want nothing to do with you. Ever." She could feel the tears of her anger welling behind her eyes.

He stared at her for several moments, but she did not give him the satisfaction of seeing her bend, not in her posture nor her attitude. She could hardly believe it, but he'd said it, clear and concise as could be. A rematch with Jackson. He could die. He could spend the rest of his days in a sickbed. And she admitted to herself, even with all the anger and terror in her mind at that moment, that it was quite possible she'd fallen in love with him. There was really no other rational explanation. Well. That would have to be ruthlessly eliminated from her mind and from her heart, as she had no intention of playing the martyr and wringing her hands over his demise and her unrequited love.

"Why are you so upset?" he asked finally.

"Out, Mr. Thompson."

"You won't tell me? Haven't we been friends . . . maybe more than friends? Don't I deserve to know what has brought on this reaction?"

How could he not know that the thought of him in that ring again was making her nauseous? He seemed truly bewildered, but she could not talk to him about her fears without revealing her heart, and she would not do that. She swept past him, opened the door, and called to Mrs. Howell. James Thompson could see himself out of her house and out of her life.

CHAPTER 14

"I'm terrified, James," MacAvoy said, clinging to his arm. James looked at the hand trembling on his forearm and up at the face of the groom.

"You have to relax. The ceremony will be over in short order, and then we'll go to Elspeth's and get you a whiskey or something," James said with sympathy. His friend was white-faced and shaking. "Come on. It's time to get ourselves to the nave. I don't see Mrs. Emory being late to her own wedding."

"I don't know if I can do this."

"You don't want to marry her? Be a real papa to Mary? Bed her mother?" he whispered.

"I do. Dear God, I do," MacAvoy said.

"Good. That's what you're going to say when the priest asks you. *I do.* Come along now," James said, pulling his friend toward the door.

James barely got MacAvoy in place and facing the back of the church when the doors opened, letting in a blast of cool March air and bringing Mrs. Emory to walk regally down the aisle, little Mary at her side. He jiggled the ring in his hand, waiting to hand it to MacAvoy and worried the man would be so shaken he'd drop it and James would have to crawl around under the pews looking for it. But for now, he listened to the sermon and heard the Bible's words. *Do not urge me to leave you or to return from following you. For where you go, I will go, and where you lodge, I will lodge.*

Unbidden, Lucinda Vermeal's face floated before his eyes. He wondered what had made her so very angry that day at her new home, pushing him away from her, urging him to leave her. He didn't believe he would leave her.

When the time came in the ceremony, MacAvoy's hand was steady and his color was back as James handed him the ring. It appeared that the groom's fears were in the anticipation rather than the execution of the marriage. He watched MacAvoy kiss his bride and then pick up Mary and kiss her too. The shy child must have understood the gravity of the ceremony, though, and wrapped her arms around MacAvoy's neck. James heard her whispered, "Papa."

James followed the triumphant groom, still holding Mary, with his bride, Mrs. MacAvoy, at his side. That would take some getting used to. MacAvoy was married. James was nodding and smiling to the guests as he walked down the aisle until a set of pale blue eyes flashed at him and looked away. Ah, Lucinda, looking elegant and unapproachable in brown silk with a wide white collar.

LUCINDA WAS NOT SURE HOW ELSPETH DID IT, MAKING EVERY one of the wedding guests in her home feel comfortable, but she did. She'd commandeered staff from her mother-in-law to manage the household and kitchen duties so that her own staff could enjoy the service at the church and the festivities in her home as one of their own was married. There were laundry maids in their best dresses alongside Mr. Pendergast's parents, scions of Philadelphia society.

"I understand there's to be no formal sit-down dinner," Aunt

Louisa said as she removed her bonnet and handed her coat to a servant in the entrance way of the Pendergast home.

"Perhaps she thought it might make some of the guests uncomfortable," Lucinda said.

"Yes. I think that is why she and Mrs. MacAvoy have chosen something less formal."

The ballroom had a huge buffet table down the center of the room and small tables for two or four guests scattered around the edge of the room. Muireall Thompson was directing her younger brother, Payden, and their housekeeper's son, Robert McClintok, on how to fill their plates and juggle a glass of punch as they approached.

"Miss Thompson? Muireall?" Aunt Louisa said with a light laugh. "Do you think they will be successful making it to one of the tables with their food and drink?"

"I'm not sure. Payden has plans to tell his sister that the small plates are ridiculous and wants to know how she expects him to get enough food to fill himself."

"Mr. Thompson," Aunt Louisa said as James joined them. "You did an exceptionally good job of keeping the poor groom from fainting. He looked terrified prior to the service."

"He was, ma'am," James said and glanced at Lucinda. "But I convinced him to stand his ground."

She took a deep breath. James Thompson was handsome enough to take her breath away on any day and devastating in the dark suit and green silk vest he wore today. She'd watched him at the altar before the bride arrived, encouraging his friend, talking in a low voice to him. Aunt was right that Mr. MacAvoy had looked pale and nervous. And then he had seen his bride, and the change in him had been startling. His face lit, his eyes devouring the very demure, beautiful, and proper woman, his bride, as she made her way down the aisle. When he'd picked up the little girl and kissed her and the child had laid her head on his shoulder, every female in the church had sighed.

It was such a romantic tableau. Nothing like the furor she was feeling for the man standing beside her, crowding her and letting their arms touch. She turned without speaking and walked away. He followed her, as she knew he would. She stopped and spoke over her shoulder.

"Find someone else to follow, Mr. Thompson," she said and continued walking toward the door to the ballroom, her destination unknown.

"Lucinda. Stop." He touched her arm. "I want to talk to you."

"How embarrassing for you," she said. "I don't want to talk to you. Leave me alone."

She hurried as much as good breeding would allow, attaching herself to Elspeth's in-laws. She saw James in her peripheral vision, standing in the middle of the room, staring at her, his hands in his pants pockets, looking more gorgeous and manly than any male had a right to.

She would not satisfy him by looking at him. She would not satisfy him in any way, she thought. No more stolen kisses and caresses. She was twenty-four and the only daughter of an incredibly wealthy and influential man. She was not unattractive. She knew that men liked to look at her. She'd been kissed before. Several times. But up until the first time James Thompson laid his lips on hers, she'd have said with all honesty that kisses were nothing to be excited about. Most were boring, some too forward, some too timid, some sloppy. But not so when he kissed her. Her mind ceased functioning when he kissed her. She belatedly realized that Mrs. Pendergast had asked her something, and she had no idea what.

"I'm terribly sorry," she said. "I'm not feeling well. I'm going to find my aunt."

She and Aunt Louisa gave their thanks to Elspeth and her husband, spoke to the bride and groom for a few minutes, and walked down the street side by side, having refused several offers to see them home, although Lucinda noticed a uniformed servant trailing them.

"I was hoping to have a slice of the wedding cake," Aunt said as they walked.

"I'm sorry, Aunt Louisa. I'm not feeling well. You should have stayed."

Her aunt laughed. "I'm teasing you, dear. I don't need a piece of cake. My waistline is disappearing as it is, and Renaldo will be waiting for me soon."

"Oh."

"What is the matter? You hurried away from Mr. Thompson, and usually you are pleased to chat with him."

"I don't ever want to speak to James Thompson again," she said breathlessly. It was such a terrible thing to think, especially now, hearing herself say it aloud. She wanted to cry but would not give in until she was safely in her home in her private sitting room.

Aunt stared at her as they walked and finally began to converse on the guests at the wedding and how wonderfully romantic it had been when that little girl hugged the groom. Lucinda listened with half an ear.

Mr. Delgado's carriage was waiting outside Lucinda's house. He stepped out of the carriage and helped Aunt Louisa into it after speaking quietly to her and kissing her cheek.

"I would dearly love to see your new home, Miss Vermeal, if you would grant me a tour, but your aunt and I have an appointment to inspect a house that I am thinking of purchasing for my family and they have asked us to arrive earlier than our scheduled time. I was going to send a message to Louisa and see if I could convince her to leave the wedding party. But here you are!" He kissed her hand. "My Louisa was dearly hoping you'd make your home with us, but I understand you're looking for some . . . independence. But know that you are welcome to come to us anytime, for a short stay or a long one. Your aunt is missing you desperately."

"Thank you. And another time, Mr. Delgado, I would love to give you a tour."

Aunt blew her a kiss through the carriage door and Renaldo walked her down the stone pathway, waiting with her until her butler, Brandleford, opened the door. Mr. Delgado bowed over her hand and bid her good day.

She climbed the staircase slowly. Giselle was waiting for her and helped her remove her dress and unpin her hair from the elaborate style she'd worn for the occasion. She let her eyes close as her maid brushed through her hair. Then she dismissed her and stretched out on the chaise in front of the tall windowed doors that led to the balcony outside her rooms. She thought about James Thompson. She could not help herself. She thought about the night of the match and the sound of a fist hitting bone and his slumped and unconscious figure on the floor of the ring. She thought about his calling for her in his incoherent ramblings and let the tears run down her cheeks. She had best harden her heart to him now rather than risk loving him and losing him, even though he was not hers and never would be. And she must not love him! She could not risk it. She intended to rid herself of that ridiculous notion immediately.

She awoke from vivid and uncomfortable dreams of him when Mrs. Howell touched her shoulder. "I'm so sorry to disturb you, miss, but Mr. Vermeal is downstairs with another gentlemen. I told them you weren't feeling well, but he said he would come up to your rooms himself to see what his daughter might need."

Lucinda sat up slowly. "Thank you, Mrs. Howell. Tell Mr. Vermeal I'll be there in a few moments and have Giselle come to my room."

A few minutes later, her butler was opening the doors to the front parlor. Her father stood from the chair he'd been seated in, and Carlton Young turned from his place in front of the fireplace and hurried to her, his hands outstretched. She glanced at them and then up at his face until he dropped them.

"Miss Vermeal, it is so wonderful to see you. I have thought of our conversations many times."

"Good afternoon, Mr. Young. Papa, I'm not feeling well. Is there something I can help you with?"

"Your housekeeper informed us you'd just returned from a party of some sort. Where were you?" her father asked rather tersely. "Did you at least have a maid with you?"

"Aunt Louisa accompanied me."

"May I say you are looking particularly beautiful?" Young said wistfully.

Lucinda ignored him and looked at her father. "I'm really not feeling very well, Papa, and would like to lay down."

At that moment the door opened, and a young maid came in carrying a coffee tray. Mrs. Howell followed. "I didn't order refreshments, Mrs. Howell."

"But I did," her father said. "Will you pour, Lucinda?"

She turned to her housekeeper. "Would you please bring me a cup of tea with some willow bark stirred in?"

"Yes, miss. Right away," she said and motioned to the young maid to leave the room.

Lucinda resigned herself to a conversation, although she intended to keep it short, regardless of what her father might think. She poured coffee for both men and did not wait long for Mrs. Howell to bring her tea. She sipped the steaming liquid and tried to relax her shoulders, knowing that her headache was as much a chance event as it was a tense response to seeing James Thompson.

"Your father has plans to show me and my family some of the city tomorrow. I'm hoping you'll join us. Or perhaps we can plan an outing to dinner or the theater."

"Of course she'll accompany us!" her father said.

"Thank you for thinking of me, Mr. Young, but I . . ." Lucinda trailed off when she heard Brandleford speaking louder than usual and a man replying. She jumped from her chair and stared at the door.

"Miss Vermeal," James Thompson said as he entered the room. "I wanted to make sure that you'd gotten home safely and that you were feeling better." He looked at her father and Young. "Am I interrupting something, gentlemen?"

"You most certainly are! What do you think you're doing, barging into my daughter's home this way? Get out!"

"Papa, please. Is there something I can do for you, Mr. Thompson?"

"I've met your father on a few memorable occasions but haven't been introduced to this young pup." James looked across the room. "Perhaps an introduction, Miss Vermeal."

"Mr. James Thompson, Mr. Carlton Young. Mr. Young, Mr. Thompson."

Carlton Young walked across the room swiftly and pumped James's hand.

"The fighter? James Thompson, the fighter?"

"I am," James said.

"Lucinda," her father seethed, "have your butler bring your two largest servants to this room immediately and have this man removed."

James looked at her father, unsmiling. "If you think a pair of burly servants will do the trick, Mr. Vermeal, then please do try. It should be entertaining, but it might be dangerous for some of the more delicate pieces of furniture in this room."

"Are you threatening me, Thompson? Do you have any idea who I am?"

"You're Miss Vermeal's father. And this is Carlton Young," James said and glanced at Lucinda. "Miss Vermeal's suitor."

"I do not have any suitors, Mr. Thompson. Allow Brandleford to see you out," she said, now noticing that the butler was still standing in the doorway.

"Will you ever fight again?" Young asked. "I've read every article I can find about your fight with Jackson."

"The rematch will be on the twenty-fourth."

"It's scheduled already! I didn't know if it would ever happen. I think we will still be here in town. I'll have to talk my father into accompanying me," Young said.

"I'll send you two tickets," James said with a wry smile.

"That would be capital! Just capital!" Young said with a boyish smile and a punch in the air.

The conversation was making her nauseous in addition to having a pounding head. She could not get the picture of him, bruised and bleeding, fighting his sisters and aunt on the night of the last match, out of her head, yet she could not bear to think about it.

"My concern is Miss Vermeal's health," James said and turned to her, pinning her with his eyes. "Are you feeling better?"

She was breathless suddenly and could feel a flush climbing her neck. She could not allow him any advantage. "I am going to lie down. Good day, Papa, Mr. Young, Mr. Thompson," she whispered and hurried through the door. She heard shouting behind her and forced herself to continue on to her rooms, to safety, to peace.

* * *

DINNER THAT EVENING WAS ITS USUAL LOUD AFFAIR, JAMES thought as he ate the carved turkey on his plate. Kirsty and Payden were arguing, and Muireall was describing MacAvoy's wedding to Aunt Murdoch as she'd been feeling poorly with chills and a stuffed head and had not attended.

"Miss Vermeal was running from you as if a pack of wild dogs were at her heals today," Kirsty said as she waved her fork at him. "What have you done?"

He shrugged as if it was no concern of his when all the while he couldn't get her out of his mind. Or that Young boy sniffing around her. "I really don't know. I went to her new house last week, and she told me to leave and never come back."

"Girls are stupid," Payden said.

"What did you say to her, James?" Kirsty asked.

"We were talking about different things, everyday matters, you know," James said, unwilling to share his declaration that he had plans for the two of them with his chatty family. He would never hear the end of it.

"I'm interested to hear *your* plans, boy," Aunt Murdoch said. "Have you even been looking for a job?"

"I've got some savings."

"I'm sure you do. But you're a man, and you need a worthwhile profession. Otherwise, your pride would suffer, although pride is not something you're in short supply of," Aunt Murdoch continued with a laugh and then a cough.

"True enough," he said. "And anyway, I can't work a job while I'm training. MacAvoy's got me working out six or seven hours a day."

Kirsty's silverware dropped to her plate. "What did you say?"

"About what? Your fork handle is in your gravy."

"Is the fight scheduled, then?" Payden asked, leaning across the table.

"What are you training for, James?" Muireall asked, staring at him in her most prim fashion, her lips pursed and her fingers tight around her glass.

"The rematch. It's scheduled for the twenty-fourth."

Aunt Murdoch was shaking her head. "I'll not do it, boy. I'll not patch you up this time."

"I'll never speak to you again! Do you hear me? Never, ever!" Kirsty said with tears in her eyes as she ran out of the room.

"What's gotten into her?" he asked.

"Payden, please go help Mrs. McClintok with the dishes and the cleaning up," Muireall said.

Aunt Murdoch stood and got her cane from where it was leaning against the sideboard. She shook her head. "I won't do it, James," she said as she left.

"What has gotten into everyone?" he asked. "It's not like you didn't know this day would come. I was never going to let a draw hang over my record."

"I am so angry with you right now I can barely speak," Muireall whispered hoarsely. "No wonder Miss Vermeal has nothing to say to you."

"Do you think she's upset about me fighting?"

"You're a fool, James. She cares deeply about you, as do all of us. We watched you struggle to breathe, be stitched up, with Payden and Robbie seeing to your most personal needs for weeks."

James flushed. "There's no need to bring—"

"There is every need. Will you commit her or myself or Kirsty to caring for you for the rest of your life? Will you have us feeding you and wiping your bottom and relying on Payden to lead the family before he is ready?"

"What are you talking about?" he asked, anger building in his gut. "You're saying I'll lose this match? That Jackson will pummel me until I'm a blabbering idiot?"

She shook her head. "Do not make this a matter of competition. This is your life. We held it in our hands and in our prayers not that long ago. Don't ask us to do it again."

Muireall stood, and he watched her slowly climb the stairs in the hallway. They were angry he was going to fight again? What did they expect him to do? This was what he did! Who he was! What alternative was there anyway? Be a mason or a cemetery worker or a mill flunky? But he knew what he could do. He could take up the offer that Alexander had presented him. He could stay out of the ring and make a good living—more than a good living, he suspected.

CHAPTER 15

Lucinda sat straight up in her bed. The handle on the balcony door in her dark room was jiggling. Her heart was pounding in her ears as she stood up, groping on her nightstand for something to defend herself with. The clock on the mantel softly chimed midnight when she opened her mouth to scream, but only a choked cry emerged. She hurried to the fireplace, reaching for a poker, her gown swaying in a cool breeze around her legs as the door slowly opened.

"Help," she whispered and raised the iron rod above her head. The figure coming through the door was in darkness.

"Jesus, Lucinda. Put that thing down," James said as he closed the door behind him.

"James?" she asked in a shaking cry. She held a hand to her breast and began to cry in earnest. "What on earth are you doing here? You've frightened me!"

"I'm sorry I scared you, but I have to talk to you, and you won't stand still long enough for us to have a conversation."

Lucinda shrugged into the robe over the back of the chair near the fireplace and sat on the edge of her bed, dabbing her eyes with a hankie and trying to slow her breathing. It was then she realized that James Thompson, a man, was in her bedchamber in the middle of the night and that she was in her gown and night rail.

"You must leave immediately," she said.

He knelt before her, on his haunches, his hands hanging loosely over his knees. "I'm not leaving until you talk to me."

"I don't want to talk to you. You must go."

"Why won't you speak to me, Lucinda? What have I done? I'll make it right."

Fear had quickly been replaced with anger. "You can't make it right, you foolish man. I am done with you. Don't embarrass yourself, and me as well, by begging. It is unseemly."

HER FIGURE IN THE MOONLIGHT SHINING THROUGH THE window as he'd opened her door was ethereal with her filmy white gown swirling around her long, thin legs. He stood slowly, staring down at the volumes of pale blond hair curling over her shoulders and down her back in waves. What was he doing here? What could he have been thinking? What if a man climbed up a rain spout to Kirsty's or Muireall's room? What would he have to say then? But then, this wasn't either of his sisters.

"Please leave," she whispered.

Why *was* he here? And perhaps she was right that he was embarrassing himself. He turned on his heel and walked to the balcony door. "Lock this again when I leave."

"Why?" she asked. "It didn't stop you."

"Because. Because I want you safe."

She stood and hurried to him, shaking her finger in his face and hissing her words. "And don't you think I'm entitled to the same wants?"

He shook his head and grabbed her finger, holding it tight. "Entitled to the same what?"

Tears streaked down her cheeks. "Knowledge that you are safe too," she whispered.

"Don't cry, love. I can't take it when you cry," he said and put his hands on her shoulders.

"I don't want to cry. But I am worried that is all I'll ever do if you don't stay away from me."

He pulled her tight against him, kissing the top of her head and wiping her cheeks with his palms. He murmured soothing words in her ear until she quieted and took a long, deep breath. She gazed up at him, her lashes glistening in the moonlight, her lips parted. There was nothing between her skin and his hands but a froth of silk and lace at her back and waist. He bent his head and touched his lips to hers.

He ran his tongue around the edge of his lips until she relaxed in his arms, her breasts tight against his chest and her legs between his. He thrust his tongue into her mouth, wanting to thrust his hips as well, but the moment wasn't about sex, although he thought of climbing over her with regularity. And if this moment with his hands on the bottom of this beautiful women and his tongue in her mouth was not about sex . . . then what was it about?

Lucinda chose that moment to lift her slender arms, the silk sleeves falling back to her shoulders, to wrap her hands around his neck. She moved her hips against his cock, which was already at full attention. She moaned at the contact and ran her finger around his ear.

He wanted her. He wanted her more than any other woman he'd ever known.

"Lucinda," he whispered and pulled her hands from around his neck, gathering them in his. "We're in some dangerous territory here. I think I should go."

"I think you should too, but not before you lie down on that bed with me. You're the only man I've ever wanted."

"You'll live to regret it." He kissed her forehead. "I'm just a run-down fighter, and I don't want to be the cause of anyone's regrets. Most of all yours."

"A woman's virginity, her body, is her own. It's not a man's to take. It's hers to give," she said, meeting his eyes in that calm and precise way that she had. She stood on her tiptoes to kiss him, running her tongue over the chip in his tooth and making him growl with need.

"I can pleasure you without taking your virginity," he whispered.

She took his hand and led him to the bed. She shrugged off her robe and bent to grab the hem of her gown, pulling it over her head and leaving her fully naked in front of him.

"I want it all," she said. "And I want it with you."

He pulled his shirt over his head and kicked off his shoes, all without taking his eyes from her body. She was slender, with full breasts, pink-tipped and puckered, curving hips, and a thatch of pale blond hair between her legs. She was the most beautiful woman he'd ever seen, with a body that would tempt a priest, and it was all bared for him. He felt gifted. He knew she was a virgin, and he was certain she did not do this lightly. He hopped around on one foot to pull off his stockings, and she looked at him with a raised brow.

He slowly unbuttoned his pants, his cock springing free, and pushed them down his legs. She was staring at him, at his crotch, and taking shallow breaths. She reached out a hand and touched him there, and he closed his eyes and moaned. She glanced up at him and sat down on the bed, inching back and stretching out until she was reclined, one knee bent, her hands at her sides.

James lay down beside her, kissed her open-mouthed, and palmed her breast, his member laying heavily on her thigh.

His body was everything Lucinda had anticipated. She'd seen his broad shoulders, deep chest, and large muscular arms when she'd watched him box and knew he was beautiful and masculine with a scattering of dark hair across his chest narrowing down to his stomach. But the rest of him made her breathless and damp between her legs.

"Do you understand what . . . ?" he asked while running a finger down her side and over her hip.

She nodded. "Aunt Louisa told me in very plain language when I was eighteen. She didn't want me to be a victim because I didn't understand a man's intent."

He leaned close to her, propped on his elbow, and hitched a smile on one side of his mouth. "And what is my intent?"

"Your intent is to take this," she whispered and wrapped her fingers around him, causing him to close his eyes and pant a breath. "And put it inside me. And then rock back and forth on your knees, moving it in and out, and in and out, until you spill your seed in my body."

"Jesus, Lucinda. You can't talk like that and expect me to hold back," he breathed in her ear.

She laid her hands on his cheeks. "Don't hold back, James."

He climbed over her, resting his weight on his forearms, kissing her and rubbing his chest against her nipples. She wanted this. She knew there would be heartache, whether she never saw him again after tonight, or God forbid, she was with child, or if he died in that boxing ring, but she would never regret it and had realized as much in a blinding moment of clarity when he'd turned to leave her—this may be the only time in her life she would be able to make love to someone because she had been fooling herself to think she didn't love him desperately. She did. No rational thought or wisdom lessened love and the heartache that sometimes came with it. Hearts made decisions without the benefit of the mind.

He spread her thighs with his knees, their eyes locked on each other. He moved himself to her entrance, teasing her with light strokes and moving his tongue in her mouth in rhythm as she sucked on it. She pulled her knees up his legs, feeling the coarse, dark hair there, and tilted her hips in invitation. They were both breathing heavily, his chest chafing at her breasts when he finally pushed himself inside, completely inside, and began to slowly thrust into her. She groaned and clawed at his back, grinding her hips to his. She was bucking wildly then, without any of her usual reticence. She was lost in the sensuality and the sexuality and the oneness. They were intimately connected, and it was the most wondrous, exciting thing she'd ever experienced.

"Harder, James, oh God, harder," she cried.

"I've wanted to do this since I danced with you that first night," he panted in her ear, his breath warm and moist. "God. I wanted to fuck you so bad. Oh. God."

That word, that dirty word, sent her over the edge, tumbling into nothingness, and she relaxed and opened, her legs and arms splayed against the mattress, the bed rocked and groaned with his weight and movement until he tensed and arched, and she felt a flood of warmth inside her. He dropped onto her, his weight hot and sensuous.

He looked at her and opened his mouth to speak. She covered his lips with her finger. "Don't say anything, James. Don't say anything at all."

She closed her eyes, suddenly exhausted and overwhelmed. When she awoke, he was gone.

* * *

"Ninety-nine. One hundred," MacAvoy shouted.

James flopped down onto his belly, his arms shaking, waiting for MacAvoy to lift the sand-filled bag from his back. He pulled in deep breaths, listening to the beat of his heart and feeling it slow down its pounding rhythm.

"That's it for today," MacAvoy said. "This is the last of the long workouts. I'm at the mill tomorrow, but you should only spend a few hours in the gym. Nothing in the ring, just work the hanging bags. And Friday will be stretching out those muscles and some sprints. You're ready for Saturday, James."

James stood and looked at MacAvoy. "I didn't realize I'd let myself get out of shape. I'm not breathless any longer after your trainings. I am ready for Saturday. Any word about Jackson?"

"Just that he'd gone back to New York to train. I would think he'd be coming back here soon. Maybe today."

James dried his face with the towel MacAvoy handed him and looked up at his friend. "When are you going to tell me about the honeymoon?"

MacAvoy's cheeks reddened as he smiled. "It was wonderful. Like something out of a dream. The hotel was fancy, and they treated us like we were really somebody. We took walks around the town—Eleanor likes to shop—and went to a musicale and had all of our meals prepared for us. I'll never forget it. Not a minute of it."

"Any minutes particularly memorable?"

MacAvoy shrugged and looked away, his ears reddening to match his cheeks. "It wasn't just, you know, fucking, if that's what you're asking about. It was more than that. Something special." He looked at James and cleared his throat. "I'm hoping I started a child in her, James. You and I were mostly concerned with stopping that from happening when we were young and bedding every female who'd let us. I don't feel that with Eleanor. I didn't once, you know, pull out, or wear a skin or anything."

"Is there any chance you succeeded?"

"Well, I gave it my best on plenty of occasions."

James laughed at his smiling friend, who was clearly pleased with himself and his new bride, watching him leave the gym with a swagger he'd not seen before in MacAvoy. That was what it was like to bed a woman, one you desired, desperately, as often as the both of you wanted. But not just any woman. She would have to be special, like Eleanor was to MacAvoy. Lucinda's face in the throes of her passion for him came to mind and even though there'd only been the one time, he wanted to make love to her often and forever.

He was not sure he would ever be interested in another woman in that way. How could he be? Whoever she was would not be Lucinda, his woman, who, for all her formality, had abandoned all her reserve in bed. But how could a woman so far superior to him ever be his?

He was still thinking about her when he walked from the alley into the kitchen of the Locust Street house. Mrs. McClintok was stirring something in a pot that smelled delicious, and he could hear chatter in the front of the house.

"Hands off the cake, Mr. Thompson. It's for tonight's dinner."

"Are you mad at me too?"

"Hmmph."

James wandered through to the parlor, where his aunt, brother, brother-in-law, and all of his sisters were gathered. "Are we having a family meeting no one has told me about?" he asked, smiling at each of them.

"Are you ready for Saturday, James?" Payden asked.

"I am," he said and sat on the arm of Kirsty's chair. "I am in the best shape of my life."

"I'm sure your opponent is in fine shape as well," Muireall said, pulling a needle through her embroidery.

He looked at Alexander. "Will you be there? Your father and uncle too?"

"We will. I'll be in your corner with MacAvoy."

"What?" Kirsty screeched. "How could you, Alexander? Elspeth! Can't you stop your husband?"

"Asking Alexander to stay away would not stop this fight," Elspeth said. "The only person who can stop this fight is James. And I personally feel better knowing there are *two* men with our brother to talk some sense into him if necessary."

James chuckled darkly. "It is comforting to know my family has so much faith in me."

Kirsty, Elspeth, and Aunt Murdoch all protested loudly that they had faith in him, but they thought he was a numskull, at least according to Kirsty, all the same.

"What does Miss Vermeal have to say about your match, James?" Muireall asked.

He shrugged. "I wouldn't know. I've not discussed it with her."

"That's because she won't speak to you," Kirsty said. "Not because she doesn't have an opinion."

"I am below Miss Vermeal's notice. Undoubtedly, she has much to keep her occupied other than a ragtag boxer," he said, feeling some bitterness creep into his voice.

"I think you're wrong, James," Elspeth said. "I think Miss Vermeal is very worried. I think she cares deeply about you."

He shook his head, and Muireall picked up the argument. "You did not see her when you were injured before. For all her outward calm, she was terrified."

He wondered if that was what had prompted her to lead him to her bed. She'd gone from shaking an angry finger in his face to making love to him as if it were the last time she'd ever see him. He thought it was likely he'd fallen in love with her. He was certain of it, in fact. And what could he possibly do about that? How could his future include her? Because he really did not think that he wanted to live without her, and he was certain she did not want to live with a man in constant danger of having his brains scrambled.

CHAPTER 16

James's fight was the following day and Lucinda intended to spend much of today with Aunt Louisa to keep her mind off him having his brains scrambled, as his aunt would say. But as she was dressing with Giselle's help, she heard a commotion in the entryway and sent her maid to see what was going on, hoping it wasn't Carlton Young asking her to join him on some outing, which he'd done three times the previous day. Thank God James was not nearby. She'd heard the derision in his voice when he called Carlton her suitor.

But perhaps it was worse. It was her father.

"Do not harass my servants, Papa," she said as went into the parlor.

"The only person I am here to harass is you," he said. "It has come to my ears that you snuck out of our home and went to see that ruffian, that James Thompson, fight. Let alone that an arena such as that is no place for a lady, especially my daughter, but that you would risk your reputation over a man such as he."

There was no use denying the fact, and it was imperative that she stood her ground. "I did go see the fight. It was horrific by any measure."

"And barbaric! I've been told they fight without all of their clothing! For a young, unmarried woman to see such a display. I'm ashamed of you, Daughter."

"I'm sorry to hear that, Papa."

"I want you to give up this . . . this," he said and swung his arm around the room, "this ridiculous notion of living away from your family home and my influence. Clearly, you still need my guidance."

"I will not. I have the money from Mother's side of the family coming to me soon and have seen a reputable attorney to safeguard it from you and your machinations."

"Machinations? That is what you call fatherly concern? Love for a daughter?"

"I do believe you love me, for all of your bluster, and I love you dearly, but I am not a child. I intend to live my life as I see fit and to have the friends I wish to have."

He plopped down onto a chair and stared up at her. He looked old, suddenly, and tired.

"I have considered writing you out of my will," he said finally. "But I'm not sure it will change your course of action."

"It will not, Papa."

"What is it? What have I done to deserve this behavior?"

She dropped to her knees and took his hands in hers. "You have done nothing except provide me the finest of everything: a good education, a secure home, and most of all, your love. But I'm no longer a child. You left everything behind, against your parents' wishes, according to Aunt Louisa, and came to America. You chose to live your life in the best manner you could."

He looked at her and shook his head. "Louisa should have never told you about my disagreements with my father. And in any case, we settled the matter quickly once he began to see the advantages of having his son in the New World. But I am a man, Lucinda."

"Times are changing. There are women in all sorts of fields

now. In academics, in medicine, in art. By the time I am forced to take over the reins of the Vermeal interests, women will be more commonplace in industry, especially once the right to vote comes for women. I will have an exceptional advantage with the foundation you and your father laid, established contacts in business and politics, and a family name that people trust. I believe we will be successful beyond our wildest dreams and have been hoping you will soon begin to tutor me in some of our business ventures. But you will never do that if you only see me as a child."

"I thought you wanted nothing to do with Vermeal businesses. You've resisted my choice for a husband, and you are reluctant to listen to me, Lucinda."

She nodded. "Yes. In the matters of the heart, Papa. But that is not all I am. I am not only a woman looking for a man. Of course I will follow your counsel in business matters. But I am a Vermeal in my own right."

His eyes widened and he looked away, turning her hands over in his and squeezing them gently. "I'm not sure I am ready for this."

"I'm certain you are. You have always been on the leading edge of finance and industry. A daughter at your side will not impede you in the least once you have had some time to settle it in your head."

"When you say things like that, you remind me very much of your mother." He kissed her forehead. "She would be terribly proud of you, you know."

"Would she? Would she be proud?"

"Absolutely," he said. "I miss her very much."

"Of course you do, and even more so with me here and Aunt Louisa ready to marry Mr. Delgado. Mama would want you to be happy. Aunt Louisa said she loved you very much. She would not want you to be lonely."

He stood and helped her to her feet. "I will take myself away from here now, as I have no interest in any matchmaking at my advanced age." She walked him to the door and kissed his cheek. "I do intend, though, to have a number of hefty male servants assigned here. You cannot expect poor Brandleford to throw out inappropriate suitors on his own, can you?"

"No, Papa. I cannot," she said and smiled at him.

* * *

JAMES TOOK A WALK SATURDAY MORNING JUST AS THE SUN WAS peaking over the horizon. He needed to clear his head, and he'd come to some decisions. Yesterday, he'd had a long discussion with his brother-in-law and had given Alexander the account numbers to access all the money he had saved and the location where the rest of the gold coins from Scotland had been hidden in the house. He'd gotten his affairs in order, as the saying went, but there was one final piece he needed to conclude, and he soon found himself staring at Lucinda Vermeal's home.

He rapped with the knocker after a few moments of indecision. Her butler finally opened the door, looking as though he'd pulled on his jacket in a hurry. He imagined he'd interrupted the servants at their breakfast.

"Would you make sure Miss Vermeal receives this?" he said.

Brandleford looked down at James's hand holding the letter he'd finalized the previous evening after several drafts.

"I put you in an awkward position with your mistress the other day. I'm sorry about that," James continued.

"Yes, sir," he said finally. "I'll see that Miss Vermeal receives it."

"Thank you."

James blew a breath as he walked down the stone walk. He'd *written* some things in that letter that, for as glib as he could be, he could not *say*. It was done now. He could hardly go back and tear the letter from the butler's hand and rip it to shreds. And anyway, he had to get ready for tonight. He had to be at his best. For himself, his family, and for his future.

LUCINDA LAY IN BED THAT SATURDAY MORNING THINKING about the evening, when James would step into the ring. She was terrified for him, but she knew there was no telling him what to do or how to live. She detested that part of his character as much as it made her admire him. He was his own man.

"Miss Vermeal?" Giselle said as she came through the door from Lucinda's dressing room. "Mrs. Howell is wondering if you would like any of the breakfast that has been laid out."

"Please tell her that just tea and some toast here in my room would be sufficient. And tell the kitchen I don't think I'll be wanting any luncheon either. Perhaps just some soup or whatever Cook has made for the staff."

Giselle returned with her tea and a message that there'd been a letter for her hand-delivered to Brandleford. "He said he told the gentleman that he would put the letter into your hands himself and will not allow me to carry it to you," Giselle said in a huff.

Lucinda smiled. "Then you'd best get me dressed so I may retrieve it."

She was not smiling when she sat down in her office, holding the letter, staring at it as Brandleford told her that Mr. Thompson had delivered it early that morning, not long after seven.

"Thank you, Brandleford," she said softly. "I'd prefer not to be disturbed."

"Yes, miss."

She stared at the envelope for some time, running her finger over her name. She broke the seal and pulled the letter out.

LUCINDA,

My sisters tell me that the reason you are angry with me is because of tonight's fight. They are angry with me as well and frightened too. I wanted you to know that I don't dismiss your fears and am glad you're concerned about me. I've done everything in my power to prepare for tonight, both physically and mentally, this letter being the final piece of that preparation.

I'll be making some changes in my life after tonight, which I'm hoping to announce if I am the winner, but regardless of the victor, I'll still be making those changes, perhaps just not as successfully. My future must coincide with my age, abilities, and opportunities. But tonight, even as you may detest the violence, I'll be fighting for you, landing every punch, for you alone.

You've captured me, Lucinda, and gifted me yourself. I love you. I'm not good at saying those types of things out loud, but it does not change the facts. I love you. Whatever happens tonight, know that you are my North Star, the shining light that guides me and makes me a better man.

Your servant,

James Thompson

"YOU FOOLISH MAN," SHE WHISPERED. "YOU FOOLISH, FOOLISH man."

She pulled a clean sheet of stationery from her desk and wrote a quick note. She handed it to Brandleford after leaving her office.

"Please get this to Mr. Laurent, the butler at my father's home, and ask that he reply as soon as he can."

"Right away, miss."

* * *

JAMES LAY ON THE FLOOR OF THE DRESSING ROOM IN THE warehouse where the fight would take place. Chambliss had changed the venue, smelling the chance to sell twice as many tickets as he usually did. It was a large empty space where a ring had been built and seating had just been completed, if his ears did not deceive him that the workmen were packing their tools. He closed his eyes, letting the sounds around him drift away, allowing his shoulders and legs to relax against the cool stones. He concentrated on clearing his mind, focusing on the visions behind his eyes. Of Lucinda as she looked up at him as he made love to her. He breathed deeply and slowly, calming his mind, freeing his thoughts from everything but his performance in the ring and who it was ultimately for. He loved her and he'd told her. If he died, if he was not right in the head after the fight, at least she would know.

But he also let his mind picture the grueling exercises, the pain, how he'd pushed his body past his own endurance. He was ready. Jackson was a formidable opponent, but he was prepared to stay on his feet and go the distance. It was all for her in any case.

MacAvoy opened the door. "It's time, James."

* * *

SHE PACED FROM ONE END OF HER PARLOR TO THE OTHER, occasionally stopping to sit down and try and convince herself to glance at a fashion sheet or read a few pages of a book. But she could not do it. Laurent had confirmed that his cousin Michael would pick her up tonight in time to see the entire bout. She did not want to arrive late or have to fight her way through crowds, although she might have to.

Brandleford opened the door to the drawing room just then. "Mr. Vermeal has arrived."

"Oh," she said, wondering how she would get her father out the door before Michael showed up.

"Come along, Lucinda," Henri Vermeal said from the doorway. "Laurent's cousin is outside with that rickety contraption he calls a carriage."

"Papa?"

"Yes, Daughter. I will not allow you to go alone. I am coming with you. Where is your cape?"

* * *

"CHAMBLISS HAS A FULL HOUSE TONIGHT," MACAVOY SAID TO Alexander. They were waiting for the rest of the crowd to file in, as Chambliss had agreed to close the doors once all the ticket holders were inside. It would have been too dangerous if standing spectators were allowed in. Chambliss would be shouting through a speaking trumpet when announcing the fighters and still might not be heard at the back of the crowd.

"My father put five hundred dollars on James tonight," Alexander said.

MacAvoy looked at him. "That's a hefty sum."

"You don't think he's going to win?"

"I absolutely think he's going to win. It will be even at first, but Jackson is going to wear down before James. I guarantee it."

"Can't guarantee an outcome. One lucky punch . . ." Alexander began.

"He's going to win."

Alexander smiled up at MacAvoy. "You're absolutely right. He's going to win."

Chambliss went to the center of the ring to make his announcements, and the crowd quieted, as he encouraged late comers to place additional bets. MacAvoy and Alexander crouched down at their corner. Seating had been built farther away from the ring than was Chambliss's usual, leaving a ten-foot-wide space between the ropes and the first row of spectators.

"The rematch of the century begins tonight," Chambliss shouted through the horn as he turned in a circle, and the crowd surged to their feet.

"First, our challenger, Johnny Jackson!"

The crowd cheered wildly as Jackson came toward his

corner through the gap between the elevated stands. He tied his colors at his corner, and Chambliss waited until the room quieted.

"And now, the man you've all been waiting for, our Philadelphia champion, none other than James Thompson!"

MacAvoy and Alexander jumped to their feet, cheering and whistling. James was staring straight ahead at the face of his opponent, without even seeming to hear the deafening roar of the crowd. He rolled his neck once and bent to step between the ropes. He held a piece of fabric, kissed it once, and tied it to the corner stake.

"That doesn't look like the Thompson plaid," Alexander shouted to MacAvoy.

"No, it doesn't. It looks like something from some woman's fancy nightie."

"Lingerie?" Alexander asked and then scanned the crowd behind him. "There, MacAvoy. She's here, and she's looking like she recognizes that strip of fabric."

MacAvoy turned and spotted Lucinda Vermeal, her eyes wide and her hands over her mouth. Her father sat beside her, staring at her. MacAvoy looked at Alexander, and both men laughed before turning to their fighter.

"Take a drink, James," MacAvoy said as Alexander held up a ladle of water. "Then put in your mouthpiece."

James drank and took the cloth from MacAvoy's hand, fitting it over his teeth.

"When I tell you to take a knee, you're going to take a knee," MacAvoy said and looked at Alexander. "Got your watch? Tell me at two minutes."

JAMES TURNED TO FACE THE OPPOSITE CORNER. CHAMBLISS rang the bell, and James charged. Both men landed furious and powerful combinations of punches to their opponent's face and midsection. Neither man stopped, both staying in the middle of the ring, throwing fists and grunting.

"One minute forty-five," Alexander shouted as Jackson caught James on the chin, spinning him around. He recovered his feet quicker than expected by Jackson and doubled the man over with two hard punches right above his navel.

"Knee, James. Take a knee," MacAvoy shouted and James dropped to one knee. He jumped up quickly and came to his corner. Alexander pulled the fabric out of his mouth and held the ladle to him. James drank while MacAvoy wiped the sweat from his face and chest.

"Dance, James. Make Jackson come after you."

James went to the scratch in the center of the ring, bouncing on the balls of his feet. When the bell rang, James threw less punches and kept himself just out of Jackson's reach, stopping occasionally to spar and then dancing away again.

"Six minutes," Alexander shouted.

"We're going to hold off another two minutes or so! James looks fine, and I think Jackson is starting to get winded."

At nine minutes, MacAvoy shouted. "Take a knee, James."

He took a knee, jumped to his feet, and headed to his corner. He drank water, and Alexander wiped the blood from his eye that was quickly swelling.

"Just another minute or so, James," MacAvoy shouted. "When I call 'now,' go after him with everything you have."

The bell rang, and James stayed light on his feet, dancing in and out of range while Jackson chased him from corner to corner. Both men landed a few punches. Jackson's mouth was bleeding heavily, and James's eye was nearly swollen shut.

"Now!" MacAvoy shouted.

And then the crowd was on their feet as James rained blows on Jackson, crowding him and punishing him with fast and cruel punches to the chin and to his midsection when Jackson raised his fists to cover his face.

"You can barely see his fists, they're flying so fast," Alexander shouted over the roar of the crowd stamping their feet and chanting, 'Thompson.' "Thirteen minutes."

"Go, James, go," MacAvoy shouted again. "Fin. Ish It."

James, sensing his opponent's weakened state, doubled the speed and power of his fists. This would be all he could give if Jackson did not go down.

James hit him hard with a left uppercut, Jackson's head bouncing back on impact, followed by a roundhouse right to the jaw. Jackson spun on his heel and dropped. Chambliss hurried to the center of the ring and counted off, waiting for Jackson to stand. He managed to get to his knees but dropped back to ground within moments.

Chambliss held up his trumpet with one hand and James's arm with the other. "Your champion, the bareknuckle champ of Philadelphia and all these United States, James Thompson!"

MacAvoy dropped to his haunches, wiping his eyes with his sleeve while Alexander shouted and danced, slapping MacAvoy on the back. The crowd stood and cheered for five long minutes while Chambliss held James's arm above his head, turning to each section of stands.

Lucinda watched as James was turned to her section, her hands over her mouth, tears running down her face. Her father was still shouting and cheering and, strangely, shaking hands with all the men around them. James was alive! He was on his feet, and he was the victor! Nothing like that horrific night from months ago.

James spoke to Chambliss, and the promoter handed James the trumpet. He pulled a wad of fabric from his mouth and lifted the speaker.

"Tonight," he said, and the crowd cheered wildly again. "Tonight is a special night for me."

MacAvoy was signaling the crowd to quiet down, and amazingly they did. "Tonight is the last time you'll see me in the ring. This was my last bout," he said to boos from the crowd. "I'm retired now after defeating Johnny Jackson, surely the best fighter I've ever faced. I'm fortunate to have always had the best cornerman in the business, Malcolm MacAvoy, at my side, and tonight was no different."

The crowd screamed louder still, and James shook his head. "It's time. It's time for me to move on to a new career. But you'll see me soon at the Thompson Gymnasium and Athletic Studio. With my partners, we intend to build the finest arena on the East Coast for training and matches. Watch your newspapers for the opening!"

He looked at her then. She knew he was looking at her. She stepped out of her seat, between the two men seated in front of her, and walked toward the ring. She could not help herself.

The crowd was cheering wildly again, but she could tell what he was saying to her even though no words passed his lips. "I love you," she said. "I love you."

He smiled that half smile that always gave her butterflies in her stomach, even with a bleeding lip. She walked to where the sash of her robe was tied to a stake.

"Have you been looking for that, love?" he asked over the din.

She nodded and reached her hand toward his outstretched ones. He kissed her knuckles, and the roar was deafening.

CHAPTER 17

"Pass the potatoes, please, Miss Vermeal," Payden said.

"She is Mrs. Thompson now, you little troublemaker. You should know since you stood up with Malcom and Alexander at our wedding," James said.

"I still think you should have set the date right after the Jackson match. That black eye of yours would have been perfect with your kilt," Payden said.

"Payden," Muireall said. "Wipe your chin and mind your manners."

"But I don't see what the problem would be for me going to Scotland. Surely, those terrible men who kidnapped Elspeth are in prison. And how would they even know I was going?" Kirsty asked, leaning forward and looking around the table.

"Absolutely not," James said.

"We've discussed this, Kirsty," Muireall said and cut her roast beef. "Cameron Plowman is still a threat. My letter from Scotland, from just a few months ago, said he was ignoring the court's orders and showed no intention of leaving Dunacres."

Lucinda watched and listened to the interactions during the meal. She was still a bit overwhelmed with the number of conversations and how each and every one of them sitting at the table managed to have an opinion on every subject possible, including those that didn't sit at the table, as the Thompson housekeeper, Mrs. McClintok, made her feelings known by withholding extra dumplings or dessert for Payden when she thought necessary.

Sometimes she missed the regularity of the quiet and politely boring meals with her father. But she would admit to herself that she loved the conversation and the laughter and even the occasional argument to be found at the Thompson table. She loved it, and she loved the man beside her. They'd only been back in Philadelphia for a few days after a two-week honeymoon, and it felt very good to be home, even though her time with James at a remote lodge in New York for a week and then a second week in New York City had been an eye-opening experience. Lovemaking was not confined to after dark or even to a bedroom.

James picked up her hand where it lay beside her plate and kissed her fingers, even as he argued with Kirsty. She glanced at Elspeth, who was smiling at her shyly, likely recognizing the depth of her brother's feelings, even as her own husband's arm lay across the back of her chair, his fingers occasionally brushing her shoulder. Lucinda had come to accept that her alone state, that she'd always believed was her preference, was only a result of not yet meeting a man she could love and who could love her.

They rose to leave after this lengthy Sunday meal and began the family's ritual of hugging and kissing each other. It was extraordinary, in Lucinda's opinion. Even if they would see each other the following day, they kissed and hugged their good-byes, and her husband did not miss any of his sisters, kissing Aunt Murdoch with a loud smacking sound and grabbing his brother from behind, Payden's arms pinned down beneath his, and picking him up. Muireall was shouting to put Payden down before he knocked something over or put his foot through one of the dining room windows. She was laughing along with Kirsty and Elspeth. All of them kissed her as well, and even though she could not bring herself to initiate it, she hugged them back. It didn't feel natural yet, but she thought perhaps it would someday.

James was helping her with her coat in the foyer while Alexander was helping his wife. Payden stared at Elspeth's stomach.

"Your coat's not going to fit much longer," he said with a grin.

"I believe you're right, Payden. I've got three more months to go until your niece or nephew arrives. And don't think I won't be making you and Robert come play with him or her when they're older, and when I have afternoon plans."

"I cannot wait to see you like that," James whispered in Lucinda's ear.

"Behave," she said over her shoulder.

"Don't forget our meeting tomorrow, James. I'll be by your house at eight," Alexander said as he guided his wife down the steps.

"I'll see you then," he said.

"Is this the meeting with Alexander's father and uncle?" she asked as he handed her into the carriage.

"It is. We're to meet with a man who has been scouting locations to purchase."

"My father is interested in investing."

"I already live in his house and ride in his carriage; I'll not work for him too, Lucinda," he said.

Once home, she found him in his dressing room, pulling off his coat. "We should hire a valet for you, dearest. You'll be far too busy to manage your wardrobe," she said.

"No. I can hang up my own clothes in my father-in-law's house."

"You are a sight when you are on your dignity, James Thompson." She handed him a thick envelope.

"What is this?"

"It's the deed to this house," she said. "My father told me he would have preferred to hand it directly to you, as he believes the husband in any marriage should manage those types of documents, but he was certain you would—now what exactly did he say? You would be an 'unpleasant ass,' and he did not want to argue with you."

HIS WIFE—BY GOD, HE HAD A WIFE—WAS LAUGHING AT HIM without even the slightest hint of a smile. He opened the envelope and saw that it really was the deed to the house that she'd been living in, that he'd moved into after returning from their honeymoon. He had a butler. Brandleford. And maids. And more than likely, he'd have a valet before long. He blew out a breath.

"He meant it as a wedding gift," she said. "Your salary will easily pay the staff, and we'll be getting our share of Vermeal stock if I am to begin working with Father. And we'll need space to entertain."

"I suppose you'd like to stay here."

"I would. I like the neighborhood and the size of the house and garden and carriage house, although we may have to look for something larger when we have children. It will be convenient for me to begin work at the Vermeal offices. It will most likely be convenient for you once you've chosen a property for the gymnasium. It is close to your sister and to Malcolm. But I would live happily with you anywhere, James."

"Even in a two-room flat?" he asked her, knowing it was his own insecurities that made him challenge her.

She pulled the pins from her hat. "Even in a two-room flat. I love *you*, not where we live."

He caught her around the waist when she turned to leave and pulled her tight, her back against his chest, his free hand working the clasps on her jacket. He slid his hand inside, working the pearl buttons of her blouse frantically until he finally touched her breasts. It should have been more familiar, more normal to him when he touched her intimately, as they'd spent much of their honeymoon naked and in each other's arms, but every time he ran his fingers over her nipples or lifted the weight of her breasts in his hand, his breath caught, his mind blank other than the driving force to get between her legs.

"James," she moaned and dropped her head back onto his shoulder, allowing him to kiss her neck at his leisure.

He released her and she turned, dropping her jacket from her arms and slipping her blouse down. She worked the buttons on her skirt until it was loose enough to fall and take her petticoat with it. He undid his trouser placket, picked her up by her bottom, leaned her against the door to their bedroom, and wrapped her legs around his hips. He felt for the slit in her drawers.

"This is why I don't want a valet," he whispered, running his tongue around her ear.

"What?"

He smiled, knowing that Lucinda in a passioned state was not quite lucid. "A valet, love. I don't want one. He might walk in here just as I do this," he said and shoved himself inside her wet heat.

"Oh God, James," she said on a groan and pulled his mouth toward her, her hips bracing against his. "Harder."

And that was the last rational thought he had as he drove into her, her climax coming fast, bringing a shiver to her shoulders and a moan from her lips. He followed soon after, shouting his release and breathing heavily against her hair as he recovered.

He kissed her deeply. "I love you. I will try very hard to not be an 'unpleasant ass' to your father, but I can make no guarantees. I'll have to thank him, which will be difficult enough."

"Don't ever change, James," she said softly, smiling and looking into his eyes, brushing his hair away from his face. "I love you just as you are, even when you are, on occasion, an unpleasant ass."

He grinned his lopsided smile. "What a lucky man I am, Mrs. Thompson."

AFTERWORD

I hope you have enjoyed James and Lucinda's story, the second in the new *Thompsons of Locust Street* series. Please follow me on Face-Book, Twitter, or on my website hollybushbooks.com, for announcements about the next book in this series, Kirsty's story, due out in the fall of 2021.

Other American set historical romance series:

The Crawford Family Series includes *Train Station Bride, Contract to Wed*, companion novella, *The Maid's Quarters*, and *Her Safe Harbor* and tell the tales of three Boston sisters, heiresses to the family banking fortune.

The Gentry's of Paradise chronicle the lives of Virginia horse breeders and begins with Beauregard and Eleanor Gentry's story, set in 1842, in the prequel novella, *Into the Evermore*. The full-length novels are set in the 1870's of the next generation of Gentrys and include *For the Brave, For This Moment,* and *For Her Honor*.

Reader favorites *Romancing Olive* and *Reconstructing Jackson* are American set Prairie Romances and *Cross the Ocean i*s set in both England and America.

Politics & Bedfellows and *All the News* are my general fiction titles published under Hollis Bush.

Please leave a review where you purchased *The Bareknuckle Groom* or on GoodReads or other social sites for readers. Thank you so much for your purchase. I love to hear from readers!

The first few pages of *Into the Evermore* and the third book in this series, the yet untitled Kirsty's story follows.

All the best,
Holly

EXCERPT FROM KIRSTY'S STORY

July 1870

Philadelphia Harbor

Chapter One

"Wait," Kirsty Thompson shouted as she hurried across the deck of the steamer Maybelle. "Wait! Stop!"

A uniformed man with sideburns that reached his chin turned from directing sailors. "Miss?"

"You must stop moving the boat," she said breathlessly, coming to a halt in front of him.

"It's a ship, not a boat," he said impatiently.

"It doesn't matter what you call it, you must stop, set the break or whatever, because I need to get off.

"I'm sorry, miss. The lines have been pulled. We'll be underway any moment now."

"But I must get off," Kirsty repeated, feeling a rising panic.

The man eyed her. "Where's your ticket, miss?"

"I . . . I don't have one."

"Then how did you get aboard?" he asked, hands on his hips.

"Well," she said. "There was a woman going up the ramp ahead of me, a rather large woman with flowered dress that nearly blinded me, with a little dog, a child, and three or four servants."

"And you walked in with her. Hiding amongst her party," he said. "You didn't want to pay passage and you thought you'd sneak aboard."

"Of course not! I'm no thief! I just needed to speak to some-one. Just for a moment, I just needed to speak to him."

"Lovers gone bad?" the man said and turned away to shout at a sailor. He turned back and regarded her. "Well, you're stuck on this ship with him now."

"Lovers! How dare you! I am not with him or anyone and that is why I need to get off!"

"You can get off in New York harbor because that's our next stop," the man shouted back at her.

Kirsty stepped closer to the man and wagged a finger at him. "You, sir, are rude and I'm going to report you to your superiors!"

"Now see . . ."

"Miss Thompson?"

Kirsty turned quickly. "Oh, Mr. Watson. I am so glad to see you! Please tell this man to stop the boat and let me off!"

The steamer lurched from its moorings and Kirsty would have tumbled to her knees if it hadn't been for Mr. Watson catching her by the elbows.

"I'm af-fraid," he said. "That will be impos-sible. We're under-way, it seems."

"Oh, no," she said and looked up at him, feeling tears gather in her eyes. She didn't want to cry. Her family even accused her occasionally of crying to get her way which was hardly ever the case and certainly wasn't now. But she dare not blink or those tears she did not want to cry would tumble down her cheeks.

"Perhaps a cup of t-tea would help you, Miss Thompson. Allow me to take you to the d-d-dining room."

"But I must get off this boat," she said. "My family won't have any idea where I've gone and . . . and they will be so worried."

"I don't b-believe there is anything we can do until we land at New York har-harbor," he said and held out his arm.

Kirsty wrapped her arm around his and looked up at him. "Oh. Oh, no. I've embarrassed you with my shouting. Your face is quite red. I am so sorry. Please don't be angry."

He shook his head. "I'm not angry," he said very slowly.

Kirsty turned as he did towards the doors leading to the inside hallways after glancing longingly at the dock. He seated her at a small table once they were in the dining room and signaled a waiter. He nodded at her to order. She opened her drawstring bag to see what amount of money she had left after paying for the trolley that morning. She was suddenly panicked when she realized she'd have to find a way to travel to Philadelphia from New York when this infernal boat stopped, and she'd need money to do it.

"Nothing for me, thank you," she said to the waiter.

"I'll have coffee and this assortment of cheese and olives listed on your menu," he said. "The lady will have tea. Thank you."

She leaned forward. "I don't have enough money to pay for it. Surely they'll give me a glass of water."

"Miss T-Thompson. I will take care of the b-bill. Please don't worry," he said and raised his hand again as if he was calling to the waiter again.

But a young, very young, red haired man walked to their table. His face had an unsightly burn scar on one side and Kirsty did her best not to look at it as he arrived at the table. She wondered if Mr. Watson knew him.

"Clawson," Watson said. "Change of plans. You'll need to contact the Royal Academy and see about rescheduling my talk."

"Yes, sir, right away, sir."

"We'll be staying in New York overnight. We'll need three rooms at the New York Hotel."

"Three rooms, sir?"

"One for you, one for me, and one for Miss Thompson," he said and nodded to her. "Clawson? This is Miss Thompson. Miss Thompson? My assistant, Mr. Clawson."

"A hotel room? Oh, no! I'll be heading directly to home. I have to get home. My family will be frantic!"

"Miss Thompson. I d-doubt we'll be able to catch a train after we arrive. We'll have to wait until t-tomorrow morning."

"Do you always take a steamer to New York? Isn't it easier to catch the train?"

"Aah," Clawson said. "I'll need to see if our tickets can be cancelled or sold, perhaps."

Kirsty watched the young man hurry away. "What did he mean about the tickets being sold? What tickets?"

Mr. Watson stared at her and then looked up at the waiter bringing their cheese platter and pots of coffee and tea. He pulled several bills out of his wallet, handed it to the waiter, and told him to keep the change. He stirred several sugar cubes into the cup of coffee the waiter poured for him before leaving the table and looked up at her.

"Tickets for a t-transatlantic crossing."

"Why would you cancel your tickets? When were you planning on sailing?" she asked, interested to know if the date could work for her although after she arrived home tomorrow, she doubted if her older sister and brother, Muireall and James, would ever let her out of their sight.

"Tomorrow, Miss T-Thompson. This steamer stops in New York to pick up additional p-p-passengers and then goes directly to England."

"Well, why can't you go now? Has something happened?"

He stared at his cup for some time. "I can hardly allow you to t-travel by yourself, Miss Thompson. I will see you b-back to your home."

Kirsty shook her head. "No. Oh, no. You mustn't. I could not allow you to change your plans on my account."

"Have some r-refreshments, Miss Thompson. We will not arrive until after eight this evening."

Kirsty felt the blood rushing to her cheeks. "I thank you for the tea and I will see that you are paid back once we are home in Philadelphia. But you cannot tell me what to do, Mr. Watson. You are not my father or brother or any relation."

He leaned forward. "I am, however, a gentleman, and you are related to my good friend Mr. Pendergast, your brother-in-law, in fact. I could not countenance any young lady traveling alone if it was in my power to prevent it, especially as she is related to my circle of friends."

"You are not stuttering, Mr. Watson." Kirsty put a hand over her mouth as if doing so would stop her rude words from being heard. "I'm so sorry. I should never have mentioned it."

He shrugged. "S-stuttering or not, I will escort you home."

"My family . . ." she began and trailed off thinking of how terrified they would be when she did not arrive home for supper.

"We will send a t-telegram as soon as we arrive at the hotel."

"You don't understand."

"W-Will you explain it to me?"

She sat quietly for several minutes, sipping her tea and staring at the spoon she'd used to stir in her sugar. She looked up at him finally with a resolved or resigned, and serious look on her face that he did not understand from this young woman. He'd met her and even escorted her into dinner at his friend Alexander Pendergast's home who was married to her sister. She was a frivolous whirlwind of chatter on that evening, but that did not stop him from finding her the most beautiful woman of his acquaintance with a joyous light giggle that went straight to his gut. However, he was certain she would find nothing remotely interesting about him or his medical research, and the fact that sometimes he forgot to eat. His colleagues called his work brilliant. His mother called him a scatterbrain.

"There are men who want to harm us," she said. "Did you know that my sister Elspeth was kidnapped before she married Alexander? She was! She was taken from us at a grand ball at Alexander's family home!"

He shook his head, hoping she would explain. She leaned close to him, close enough that he could smell lilacs or some other aromatic that seemed to wrap around him but yet he could feel her panic.

"My father was the Earl of Taviston. There was a man, an illegitimate cousin, who claimed the earldom was his and he tried to kill my mother, stole my younger brother from us, and lobbied the governors who oversee such things in Scotland to give him the title and the wealth and the lands. My father was so concerned for the safety of his family that he brought us to America hoping to wait in safety until everything was settled and Plowman, the cousin, was jailed. But they murdered my father and mother on the passage here!" she hissed. "They poisoned their food, and they were buried at sea."

She had tears in her eyes as she whispered to him, as if there were enemies all around.

"Why did they kidnap Mrs. P-Pendergast?"

"An exchange! They wanted us to turn over my brother Payden, the heir to the earldom," she said with a trembling lip. "Elspeth knew her duty, though. She would die for him, as would any of us."

"Die for him?"

"Had Alexander and my brother James not rescued her, she would have been . . . abused and murdered as we would never turn the rightful Earl of Taviston over to them."

He sat back in his chair and stared at her. Good God! What a story!

"I thought you had an older brother," he said remembering

the looks he'd gotten from the man as he'd escorted his sister into dinner that night. He was a boxer and a champion, too.

"James? He is actually a cousin. His parents died when he was an infant, his mother was my father's sister. Mother and Father took him in and raised him as their own."

"But he's not your true b-broth . . ."

She'd leaned across the table again but there were no tears this time, only a look that would have scared the most seasoned soldier. "James Thompson is my brother."

He nibbled on some cheese and a cracker and pushed the platter to her side of the table. "So your family will assume something s-similar has happened to you."

She nodded. "When will we arrive in New York?"

"B-by eight this evening," he said and looked up at her. "Why did you come aboard?"

Her face reddened, like a length of pink gauze slowly crept up from the base of her neck.

"Well," she said and looked at her hands. "I was hoping to talk to you."

"T-To me? Whatever for?"

"Alexander said that you travel to England regularly for your medical work and I was hoping you'd agree to escort me and a companion," she said and looked up. "I plan to import fine Scottish wool and yarns to America. I believe Thompson Fabrics would be quite successful. I need to go to Scotland and meet the people I've been corresponding with about such a venture."

"Your brother would never allow it."

"No. But there would be nothing he could do, if I boarded with my companion while they read a letter about my destination."

"And you think I would have agreed to this outrageous scheme?"

"You aren't stuttering. Again."

"I find that I don't stutter when I am furious."

"Oh. What prompts it when you do stutter?"

He looked away. Miss Kirsty Thompson had the body of a siren, the face of an angel, and the scruples of the devil. He was, at the same time, horrified by her and attracted to her. Perhaps there was a medical explanation. And his stutter was especially prevalent when he was nervous. This young woman made his orderly, scholarly world tilt on its axis.

EXCERPT FROM INTO THE
EVERMORE

Into the Evermore

November 1842 Virginia

"Twenty dollars and you can have her. Don't make no never mind to me what you do with her. I just want to see the gold first."

The filthy-looking bearded man waved his gun in every direction as he spoke, including at the head of the young woman he held in his arms and at the three men in front of him. The trio all had handkerchiefs covering the lower part of their faces and hats pulled down tight, revealing six eyes now riveted to the pistol as it honed in on one random target after the other. The woman was struggling, although it was a pitiful attempt as she was clearly exhausted, and maybe hurt. The wind whipped through the trees, blowing the dry snow in circles around them. Beau Gentry watched the grim scene play out as he peered around a boulder down into a small ravine. He'd been propped against the sheltered rock, dozing, and thinking he'd best start a fire, when he heard voices below.

"Ain't paying twenty dollars in gold for some used-up whore," one of the masked men said.

The filthy man wrenched his arm tighter around the woman and put the gun to her temple. "Tell 'em, girly. Tell 'em you ain't no whore."

She shrank away from the barrel of the gun and moaned. "Please, mister. Let me go," she begged.

"Tell 'em you ain't no whore!"

She shook her head and pulled at the filthy man's arm around her waist. "I'm no fallen lady," she whispered. "I'm just, I'm just . . ." The woman went limp, and Beau thought she'd fainted but instead she vomited into the snow in front of her. He watched her choke and gag, bent over the man's arm, and that's when he realized she was barefoot.

Beau leaned back against the rock and checked his pistols and shotgun beside him. He hoped his horse wouldn't bolt from the tree she was loosely tied to when the bullets started to fly. It'd be a long walk back to Winchester if she did, especially as he'd most likely be carrying the woman. "Shit," he muttered. "Shit and damnation. She doesn't have any goddamn shoes on."

From his angle, he'd need to drop the three bandits with the two shells from the shotgun, and finish off any of them still breathing with one of his pistols. They'd be surprised and hopefully slow if the liquor smell floating on the wind meant anything. He was counting on the filthy man being hampered by the woman's struggling. He was hoping she didn't get shot in the cross fire, but then she'd be better off dead than facing what was in store for her if the filthy man was the victor. The argument over the gold was getting heated, he could hear, making this as good a time as any.

The snow fell away from the fur collar and trim of Beau's coat as he stood, lifted the shotgun to his shoulder, and aimed at the first man. He pulled the trigger, sighted in the second man, and pulled the second trigger right after the other, marching forward through brush and snow, letting the shotgun fall from his hands as he went. Two of the men dropped and the third fell to his knees, aiming his pistol at Beau as he did. Beau lengthened his stride, pulled a pistol from his waistband as he made the clearing, raised his left arm straight, and dropped the kneeling man to the ground with a shot to his face, letting the spent weapon fall to the ground. As he turned, he pulled his new fighting knife free of its scabbard and brought his right hand up, wielding a second pistol, side-stepping to get an angle on the filthy man.

"She's mine! You ain't getting her."

"Drop the gun."

"Twenty dollars in gold and you can have her!"

He wondered how much longer the woman would last. She was white-faced, except for the dirt, and her hair hung in clumps, matted together with blood. Her mouth was open in a silent scream. She raised and lowered her arms as if paddling in a pool of water. Most likely she was long past terrified and all the way to hysterical.

"Fine," Beau said. "You want twenty dollars?"

The filthy man nodded, and Beau dropped his knife in the snow and reached his hand in his pants pocket as if intending to retrieve a gold piece. The man lowered his weapon by an inch or so as his eyes followed Beau's hand, and in that moment Beau brought up his right hand and fired his weapon. The bullet tore through the man's neck, sending blood gushing into the snow as the man tumbled sideways, releasing the woman. She fell in the opposite direction, covered in splattered blood, clawing and crawling away from her captor, turning on her back and shoving off in the mud and snow with bleeding feet, pushing herself away. Her cry echoed in the silent cold night.

Beau pulled his knife from the snow, kicked away the filthy man's gun, and walked to where he lay, now writhing as he slowly drowned in his own blood. The hair on the back of Beau's neck stood and he turned. The last of the three men, missing part of his cheek and ear, had retrieved a loaded pistol from the belt of one of his companions and was now aiming it at Beau with shaking hands. Beau released the knife with a whip of his wrist, landing it dead center on the man's chest. He turned to the woman and watched as her eyes rolled back in her head and she crumbled the last four or five inches, until her back hit the forest floor.

Made in the USA
Las Vegas, NV
06 April 2021